TOUGH WOMAN RANCH

Terrence Corcoran 5

JOHNNY GUNN

D1310179

WOLFPACK
PUBLISHING
— EST 2013 —

Tough Woman Ranch
Johnny Gunn

Paperback Edition
© Copyright 2019 Johnny Gunn

Wolfpack Publishing
6032 Wheat Penny Avenue
Las Vegas, NV 89122

Paperback ISBN 978-1-64119-819-6
eBook ISBN 978-1-64119-818-9

TOUGH WOMAN RANCH

CHAPTER ONE

"Looks like some big trouble up Winnemucca way, Sheriff." Eureka County Deputy Sheriff Terrence Corcoran handed the wire back to Sheriff Ed Connors. "Comes right out and says it's the Brad Doolin outfit."

"Got it this morning, Terrence," he said, putting the wire on his desk. "Gettin' mighty brave robbin' a bank and takin' a hostage. If it's Doolin and company, they might just be headin' this way, according to Giles Murphy in Austin."

"Yup," is all the big deputy said. Gangs preyed on banks, stagecoaches, and trains that ran between Elko on the east and Reno on the west, along the old emigrant trail, and often, after a big hit, would venture south into what they considered 'safe' grounds. Eureka was a rich little county with mining companies sending gold and silver out, and bringing big payrolls in. It was a hub on a lesser used emigrant trail and had an active commercial center and bank.

The thing with Nevada, and what made it open territory for the gangs, was the fact it was so sparsely populated. Two major east-west roads and the railroad connected small villages separated by as much as hundreds of miles. There were ranches or mines, close in, north and south of those villages, and other than that the state was empty. In the vast valleys between high mountain ranges, larger ranchers took care of themselves, and outlaws had no reason to attack them, anyway.

Each village would have a bank and commercial center, usually a saloon and hotel or two, and maybe even a boarding house. The gangs could establish a well-stocked hideout and strike fast, run fast, and get lost in the vast wilderness of the great Nevada deserts. With the advent of the telegraph, the various county lawmen were able to alert each other about outlaw activity.

"Think I'll wander down to the bank and then drink some lunch," Corcoran said. "Been a long day. Anything else comes up on this, come get me. Doolin's got my dander up some, throwing an old lady in the river like that."

"How you comin' on those rustlers? Boys out in the valley gettin' their dander up."

"I'm close to putting the irons on Butch Clemons and Ed Reason. They've got a small herd in a valley east of us, and that herd has been growing fast. I'm sure they've got some nasty little runnin' irons to doctor the brands."

Corcoran stands in at about six feet two, has long wavy reddish hair, and has been carrying a badge for many years. He was born on the ship carrying his family from their home in Ireland, so despite his shenanigans about being Irish born, the man's never been there. "Only in my dreams," he likes to say. "I didn't kiss the Blarney Stone. I pinched the nurse that delivered me."

Corcoran loves the ladies, and they are quick to return

the favor. No woman will be abused if he's around and every woman is a lady until she says otherwise. His knuckles and slightly canted nose will attest to his fighting ability, and the handles of his Colt show considerable wear.

"You think Clemons and Reason have help?"

"I don't think they're smart enough to find help," Corcoran laughed. "They work the range at night, moving just two or three animals at a time. The ranchers that pay attention know their losses. The others don't discover theirs until market time. Reason's a hot-headed idiot, and Clemons thinks he's building a herd. Neither one has the common sense of dead coyote."

Ed Connors was enjoying his first week on the job. He easily won the election over a man who spent more time with the easy ladies than he did at his own general merchandise store. Connors was a busted-up buckaroo off a Diamond Valley ranch some thirty miles north of town. His campaign was a simple one and resonated with the county folk. "It is in our best interests to not break the law, and for those that do, it is in your best interests that I break them." Corcoran was one of his biggest supporters.

"Never have understood why you didn't run for sheriff, Terrence, my boy? You could have simply walked into this office." Connors was going to be very comfortable as sheriff. He didn't take guff from anyone, believed in individual freedom and would allow just about anything that didn't infringe on others.

"Well, Ed, I kinda like the idea of being a deputy. Never did cotton to paperwork, don't have a taste for politics, you know I won't lick nobody's boots, and I can run off chasing a bad boy knowing the town is safe cuz the sheriff's ta home." He laughed right out slapping his beat-up sombrero on and walking out onto the dusty street.

"What'cha putting up there, boy?" One of the town boys was tacking a poster on the wall of the sheriff's office.

"Gonna be a big dance, Mr. Corcoran, and even the kids are invited this time. You know how Mr. Henderson likes to roast calves and pigs, and all the women are making pies. You gonna dance with Cindy Payton? Or maybe Marvell Cornell?"

"You're about to get you bottom tanned, sonny. Don't never tease a man about a woman liking him some. It's a man's right to have women like him. You'll understand that someday." He handed the kid a nickel, took a swipe each way across his huge mustache and walked down the dry and dusty street. *I think I'll dance with both those lovely women. Cindy's a feisty little wench, and we have had our fun times. Marvell is too young, but a good dancer.*

Corcoran slipped into the bank to alert Peter Bridges about the Doolin Gang working the bank in Winnemucca. Bridges was in his sixties and was one of the founders of Eureka back in the sixties when silver was first discovered. It was that silver that built his bank and several other buildings in the community.

"Doolin, eh? I've heard the name, but he'd have a hard time gettin' anything from me. Don't like thieves, Corcoran, not one bit." Old timers remember Bridges in a gunfight with three outlaws looking to rob his bank. Two went to the cemetery; the third made the Carson City prison. Everyone who worked at the bank took mandatory target practice and wore a sidearm.

"Just wanted you to know. Thanks, too for that tip on Butch Clemons. He's building a herd with few heifers, and now putting money in the bank with few calf sales. Maybe we're in the wrong business, sir," he chuckled. Bridges frowned.

"Most outlaws take money from a bank, not put it in," Bridges said. "That caught my attention. Don't think the man's got a head for this outlaw business."

The Brad Doolin gang had been harassing trains and stage lines in eastern Nevada for the last several months but robbing a bank in broad daylight and taking a hostage was a big step up in Doolin's outlaw career. Moving to the north-central part of the state was also a big change for the outlaw.

"Do you suppose that hostage thing was staged, Corcoran? I mean, do you suppose that woman is part of the gang?" Peter Bridges was an old-line hard rock miner who struck it rich, but despite the money, never gave up the life. The idea of that kind of deception rang true for him. He'd dealt with high-graders in the drifts and bunko artists at the stock market.

"No, Mr. Bridges. He threw that lady off the bridge and into the river. No, she wasn't a part of it and Doolin's in a world of trouble if he comes this way. One thing I won't tolerate is a man behavin' badly with a woman. That wire says she's sixty, sir."

Bridges shook his head watching Corcoran walk up the street. "We're pretty lucky here in Eureka having Corcoran and Connors. Almost feel sorry for Doolin if he shows up around here."

Corcoran made his way up the main street of Eureka, past the brand-new opera house, and into the Bonanza Club, the oldest business in town. When silver was struck, Jimmy Henderson put up two barrels inside a wall tent and called it his Bonanza. Wooden walls followed, and the next year the tent roof was replaced with a wooden one. The Bonanza Club had grown into two stories of pleasure.

There was a saloon with gambling and a separate and fine restaurant on the lower level with boarding rooms on the upper. Henderson held one or two rooms aside for travelers, and the others were taken by a couple of working girls and a few miners. The Bonanza Club was the social center of Eureka.

If you wanted the latest gossip, the latest on the mines' stocks, or needed to understand the politics of Eureka County, you spent an hour or so in the Bonanza Club.

There were two large mining operations employing hundreds of men, the Richmond Mining Company and the Eureka Mining Company. They were seldom friendly rivals, and outbreaks of violence happened. There was also violence whenever the idea of a union came into play. That was the only time the mining companies agreed on anything.

Corcoran conducted as much sheriff business at the bar as he did at the jail and was sure to be found close by if there was trouble. Trouble, that is, caused by the fine upstanding deputy or brought under control by the same deputy. Henderson often wished Corcoran would find another drinking palace, and at other times blessed his good luck in having him for a good customer.

Henderson himself was the barman when Corcoran came through the swinging doors of the Bonanza Club. "Terrence, as I live and breathe. In for the free lunch, I presume?"

"With a flagon of cold beer, my man. Cold, if you please. See you have the Founder's Day Jubilee posters up. That should be a fun time in the old town. Guess you heard about the bank robbery? Whatcha got good to eat today?"

"Roasted beef, some fruit, and Cindy has some of her venison sausage sliced, too. Doolin is the first name come to mind, Corcoran when I heard the bank robber story. Course that might just be because he's been in the news so much lately. He kill anyone this time?"

"Nope, but I wondered about that," Corcoran said as he ambled to the long table loaded with the free lunch foods. Henderson said he got the idea of a free lunch reading about some saloons in the east featuring free lunch if you buy drinks to go with it. "Damn fine roast, Henderson. Pete Richardson lost a calf last week. This wouldn't have anything to do with that, would it?"

"You hurt me to the center of my soul when you say things like that," the big barman laughed. "I told you it was long smoked, didn't I?" He pretended to pull the knife from his heart, and Corcoran laughed. "My beef will always be better than Pete's."

Cindy Payton ran out from the kitchen and jumped into Corcoran's ready arms. "Good thing I saw you coming, girl. I would have had to make an important decision."

"Decision?" she asked, wrapping her arms around the deputy's neck.

"Yup. Whether to drop you or drop my lunch," he laughed. He carried her in one arm and his lunch in the other hand to the bar. "Best lunch I've had all week," he said. He kissed her forehead and set her down gently.

"It's Monday," she said. He smacked her bottom, and she kissed him quick on the cheek and ran back to the kitchen. "Elk stew on the stove for tonight, big guy."

"I'm gonna take a ride up the Diamond Valley, Jimmy.

Somebody's been movin' other people's cattle out there. Heard anything?"

"Butch Clemons has been in a couple of times this week looking for Ed Reason. Those two are bad trouble. Might want to check on their activities."

Before he could answer, the quiet of the midday was broken about the same as the bottle that crashed against the bar. Two miners, off the night shift and now drowning their sorrows were about to tear the place up. Corcoran took three steps down the bar, whirled one of the men around and smashed his Colt across the man's head.

As miner number one crumpled to the floor, he cocked the revolver and aimed it at miner number two's broad chest. "Pay for the bottle of whiskey, drag your partner out the door, and go home. You boys work hard enough. You don't need to whup on each other."

The hard rocker did as he was told, with the big deputy standing and watching, and Corcoran walked back to his spot at the bar, nodded to Henderson with a little grin, and grabbed his pint. He drank his beer, ate his lunch, and rode his horse out of town to find Clemons or Reason.

It was the middle of summer and the day was hot and dry. Eureka sits up on a hillside, looking west across the wide and often lush Diamond Valley, and east across a mountain range and into a canyon that empties into another wide and lush valley. The mountain range is home to deer, elk, bighorn sheep, and antelope, and is a magnet for summer thunderstorms and winter blizzards.

He was nearing the Eureka and Palisades Railroad tracks when he spotted Ed Reason near the cattle loading docks and rode over. "Need to have a few words, Reason."

"Not today, Corcoran. Busy, here," he snarled. Reason wasn't a big man, tried to look like a bad man, a dangerous man, and it didn't come off very well. He idolized real outlaws, carried his sidearm low, not like a buckaroo. Hard to ride a horse when your gun hangs off your thigh. He wore a little pencil mustache, but since it was blond, no one knew it was there.

His eyes, though, were mean. Cold with anger, and some say he took his frustrations out on his horses or the working girls at the Bonanza. Most outlaws carry scars, almost as badges, but Reason's face was clean. He wanted more than anything to be a big-time outlaw and wasn't.

Corcoran reached out and jerked the man off the chute and was off his horse standing over the inert man in half a second. "Don't look much busy, Reason," he chuckled. "Where's your partner?"

Reason dragged himself to his feet, tried to dust himself off, which looked rather humorous to Corcoran. "You had no call to do that, Corcoran. I ain't done nothing."

"You're here at the loading pens, and that's something in my book, Reason. Where's your partner? There won't be a third time." He had his fist doubled and ready to smash Ed Reason's nose flat.

"Movin' some steers down. And I gotta get up there to help."

"Whose steers?" Corcoran snarled. "Doubt you boys have enough to sell."

"We had a good year, Corcoran. Now let me go help Butch."

"Yeah, a good year. I'll be right here for the sale, Reason, and those brands better check out. One messed up brand, and you'll be behind bars or hanging high." Corcoran mounted and turned his horse to ride back to town.

CHAPTER TWO

Brad Doolin led his gang of three into a narrow canyon in the hills leading up to Golconda, a mining community some miles east of Winnemucca. "Brush out those prints best you can," he called back to Sandy Whiting. The third member of the gang, George Fountain rode directly behind Doolin. Whiting was dragging a large sagebrush behind him, trying to wipe out what prints the horses might be leaving.

"Wind'll take care of what's left," Whiting called out. "Won't be too far behind you, but don't be countin' that money till I get there." *Why do I have to do the draggin'? Is Mr. Big Shot Doolin too good to do the draggin'? I better get my full share.*

Doolin, thirty years old and a born killer, didn't respond to the jibe. Whiting was a mealy-mouthed, skinny little back-shooter who was an excellent shot with rifle, pistol, or shotgun. He was also responsible for most problems within the gang.

Like so many, Doolin came west to find his fortune, but without the hard work that usually goes along with that. He was a strong-arm thief in St. Louis, robbed banks in Chicago, and drifted into Nevada two years ago. His method was usually armed intimidation rather than simply shooting everyone around; However, there were bodies strewn about often enough. The wanted posters always called him a killer.

"I gotta put that boy in his place one day soon. Damn fool almost killed that woman."

"Happens sometimes," Fountain chuckled. "But grabbin' her wasn't necessary."

Grabbing a sixty-year-old bank customer as they fled the Humboldt Savings Bank was stupid, and Doolin planned to have it out with Whiting that night. What was worse was throwing her over the bridge and into the Humboldt River as they fled town. The gang rode north for ten miles then turned east across the broad Paradise Valley and into the Golconda district where they had a well-provisioned hideout.

"You're gonna have to calm that boy down, Brad. Lot of people will tolerate robbing a bank or two or taking bank and government money off a stagecoach, but they ain't gonna like hearing that we carried an old woman off."

"I know, dammit," Doolin spat out. "We'll have it out tonight. We need to move, also. That fool stunt is gonna bring a large posse this way, sure as hell. We can hide out south of Battle Mountain and hit those stagecoaches that run up the Reese River from Austin. Who's the sheriff in Lander County? Anyone we know?"

"Gotta think on that Brad. Lots of gold coming out of Austin and coming down from Belmont. They bring it to Battle Mountain where the railroad runs. Makes it from Utah all the way to Reno."

"Yeah, the gold is shipped north to the railroad,

George. Those are the wagons and coaches we want. Railroads is puttin' too many guards on board. That road north from Austin should make for easy pickins."

"The Lander sheriff is Giles Murphy, I think, but listen, you forget they just built that railroad from Austin to connect with the Central Pacific. They won't be no wagons haulin' gold. Probably no stagecoaches, neither."

"Didn't know about that," Doolin snarled. "We'll just go on to Eureka, then, or maybe back to Ely or Ward. Don't matter none as long as we get far away from here."

"I heard good things about the Ward district," Fountain said. "They got a lot of gold to move."

They took what appeared to be a little-used trail off the main road. It led into a long canyon that twisted and turned and eventually led east. Their shack was deep in the canyon, in a broad area that featured a spring and a ring of cottonwood trees. The small spring bubbled fresh water into a pond in the center of the ring, and the cabin and corral sat back from that. It was easily defended, and Doolin had it well stocked with food and whiskey.

"Hate to leave this place, but you're right, Brad." George grabbed Doolin's reins as they dismounted and led the two horses into a corral while Doolin took the money sacks into their cabin.

Three heavy canvas bags were flopped onto a round table near the cook stove, and Doolin went to work getting a fire started, wondering how he was going to handle the Whiting problem. *That man's got a problem that's gonna be the death of the rest of us if I don't put him in his place.* He snickered when he thought maybe he'd just shoot the fool when he walked in the door. He laughed right out when he murmured, "Maybe I will."

Coffee was boiling by the time Fountain walked in, and

Doolin poured some. "Grab that bottle in the cabinet, George, let's have a snort for our good luck in getting away today. I sure wish Sandy hadn't grabbed that old lady. They're gonna be on us like hound dogs."

"I'd just shoot the bastard, Brad. He's gonna get us killed, sure as I'm sittin' here."

"I had the same thought but real honest. Now, we need that gun of his. I want the gold from those stagecoaches, and his gun is important. Sure wish it was in someone else's hands, though," he chuckled. "Sounds like Sandy riding in now. I'll handle this some way, George."

"I'll back whatever play you make, Brad. I like riding with you."

"She gonna be okay, Sheriff?" A man on the bridge hollered down to the Humboldt County Sheriff Frank Acord. Two men were doing their best to get Clara Bentley out of the Humboldt River where Sandy Whiting dumped her. Clara was a large woman, and her wet clothing added another fifty or sixty pounds the sheriff was attempting to move.

"Better get the doctor. She's unconscious, and there's lots of blood," Acord yelled up to the man on the bridge. "Is Buford Lamb up there?" He got a nod back and yelled, "Send him down."

Lamb grew up on a Humboldt County ranch and wanted more than anything in the world to be a lawman. He read about New York and Chicago police, about European police, and when he turned eighteen, he presented himself to Acord with the comment, "I'm going to be your new deputy, Sheriff."

Acord couldn't hold back the chuckles and tried to dismiss the large ranch hand, but Lamb refused to go. "I've read the books and watched you, and I know I'll be the best deputy you got." No argument Acord used would slow the boy down, and after two days, Acord swore him in. That was six months ago, and Frank Acord wondered often how he managed his office before Buford Lamb.

Acord was in his fifties, had been a lawman for years, following the building of the railroads west, staying as sheriff or marshal in the little towns that built up, but always on the move. He found Humboldt County to his liking and has been sheriff for almost ten years. He's got a serious like for being a laid-back gentleman, letting his deputies do most of the work.

"Make sure the doctor takes care of this woman and then get your arse up to the jail. I'm putting a posse together, and you're in it." Acord hustled up the river bank and headed for the jail to gather the rest of his deputies, all two of them, and spread the word they would be hunting down the Doolin Gang.

Buford Lamb was big even by ranch hand standards. His pa, Jackson Lamb, was well over six feet and well over two hundred pounds, and young Buford was bigger, stronger, and had a quick mind and quick wit.

"Well, damn me," he muttered, climbing out of the river when the doctor arrived. "She fell more than ten feet off that bridge and hit the water flat on her back." He shook his head seeing all the blood from the bash she took to her head. "She'll live, Doc?"

Doc Graham just nodded, pushing young Lamb out of the way. "Well, then, I gotta go and catch the fiend what tossed her down here." He raced all the way back to the jail, got his horse out of the courthouse stables, made up a three-day pack for he and the sheriff. It was a quick ride to the front of the courthouse to meet the posse.

"Brought smoked meat, beans, flour, and coffee, Sheriff. Got my rifle, shotgun, and sidearm, along with plenty of ammunition. Everybody at the bridge swore it was Brad Doolin and his gang at the bank."

"People at the bank said the same thing. I wonder, though, at snatching that woman. That ain't like him. Damn fool thing to do."

"She weren't no pretty young thing that might get kidnapped, neither. Sure makes me mad thinkin' about it. We'll catch that fiend," Lamb said."

Doolin had built a reputation of robbing and stealing money and gold from banks and stagecoaches, but not for harming the victims. He killed lawmen or others who tried to interfere, but not the victims. He took pride in that, even reminded victims that they were safe as long as they provided him with their possessions. At the slightest provocation, though, he killed.

"Is this all we got? You, me, Jake, and Lester? Think we're enough?"

"All I really need is you and Jake, but Lester Thompson will lead that pack mule you brought, in case we're gone for some time, and I'll probably have to come back since you two are my only deputies." Acord wasn't looking forward to a long chase across the great Intermountain desert. "Someone has to be in town, and you two are young," he chuckled.

Golconda sits on a plateau overlooking the vast Paradise Valley to its west and northwest, with high mountains to its east. There's good water in the valley, ranches are spread along the western valley near the Santa Rosa Mountains, and gold was known to be found in the mountains east and north of the little community.

"Which way you figure they headed, Sheriff?" Lamb bailed off his horse and tied it and the mule to a rack.

"It'd be east if I was runnin'," he said. "Lots of room to hide in." Frank Acord watched his two deputies come down from the office. "He headed out north across the river, so we'll have to give close attention to finding his trail."

"It's just gonna be the four of us, boys. Buford, you and Jake ride out north across the bridge and see if you can spot a trail if they might have left the road. I don't think they'll continue on north, so keep a close eye. We'll follow along with the mule."

"I'll leave plenty of sign, Sheriff," Lamb said. "The mule has supplies for three days." He and Jake Oxford rode out while Sheriff Acord and Lester Thompson got their mounts ready for the chase.

"Why only the four of us, Sheriff?" Lester Thompson was long into his fifties, looking to pick up a small piece of property and settle back for his remaining years. He lost his wife in a fire two years ago and spent several months deep in bottles of rotgut whiskey before Acord dragged him out of the mire.

"I want to ride fast and hard, Lester. There's three of them in the Doolin Gang, and there's four of us. You keep that mule coming along behind us when we get on their trail. Jake and Buford are young and strong, and I'll give them the lead, but we'll need the supplies on that mule, so keep moving on our trail."

Thompson was glad to hear that he probably wouldn't be in a shoot-out with Brad Doolin or his gang and nodded to Acord as he mounted for the chase. "I'm with you, Frank," he muttered.

About three miles north of the Humboldt River, Acord spotted the marks Lamb left and turned out across the broad plain of the desert in an easterly direction. "Easy to follow Lamb and Oxford, but the Doolin trail is damn faint," Acord said.

"Looks like they're draggin', Frank. Old Indian trick to hide your trail. 'Course you're leavin' a drag trail," he laughed. "It works best if whoever is following is a day or two behind and the wind gets things all scattered about."

There were deep arroyos cutting across the plain that slowed progress some but also gave Doolin opportunities to hide his trail and Acord mentioned they just might be riding into a trap. "Naw, that man's got sacks of spendable money, Frank. He's gettin' out of this country, I'll bet."

It was mid-summer, hot as blazes, as they made their way through great stands of sage and rabbitbrush, wended around pine and cedar groves, and dipped in and out of arroyos. "They're riding a straight line, Frank. After dumping that woman in the river, Doolin's gotta know I'm looking to chase him down."

The valley was a natural basin feeding the Humboldt River, and many springs and tributaries meandered through it. Wild thunderstorms in the summer filled the creeks and arroyos to overflowing and allowed for good grazing grasses to flourish. "He knows where he's going, sheriff, otherwise he would have taken a road out. Jake and Lamb will have to keep their eyes open."

CHAPTER THREE

"Looks like they're heading for Golconda, Buford," Jake Oxford said as they climbed out of a deep arroyo and picked up Doolin's trail. "Wouldn't be my first choice." Oxford was a couple of years older than Lamb, and the two hit it off just right when Lamb joined the force. They were both big and strong, both held Frank Acord in high esteem, and both took great pleasure in wearing a badge and keeping the peace.

Their youth, strength, and desire to be good lawmen made Sheriff Acord's life that much easier. They knocked heads breaking up the saloon fights, they rode hard and long chasing bandits and road agents, and they brought a balance of age and youth to his office.

"Knockin' heads and flirtin' with the girls," Jake Oxford would slap Lamb on the back as they walked the busy streets of Winnemucca. "I love wearing a badge."

"Probably heading for the mountains to the north and east Jake. Lots of canyons and draws they could get into. Whoever's doin the sweepin' ain't got his heart in it.

Think Doolin's smart enough to make this a false trail? To have one of his men just ride off and sweep the trail?"

"That would be a good trick, but we have at least three horses we know for sure we're following."

The trail wasn't difficult to follow since they weren't on an existing road, and the ride was easy until they came up to the mountains north of Golconda. Sparse stands of cedar, acres of sage, and scrub piñon pine turned to stands of ponderosa pine, aspen, and cotton-wood, along with towering rock-strewn mountainsides. The trail seemed to vanish when they rode toward the mouth of what looked to be a deep canyon leading into the range.

A small creek flowed out of the canyon, its banks lined with willow, and there was a small copse of cottonwood at the canyon's mouth. They rode their horses in circles for a couple of minutes, trying to understand how all the prints and attempted brushing just ended.

"Whoever that sweeper is, Jake, he ain't got much for brains. The trail stops dead at the entrance to that canyon. Let's be nice and slow riding in there and keep separated. Those trees would sure be a good place to hide for an ambush." The entrance was somewhat narrow due to rock slides and widened as they rode in. Scrub brush and cedar dotted the canyon walls along with tumbled rock slides. It was a steady climb as the canyon widened more the higher they got.

A small stream, probably fed by numerous springs higher on the canyon's flanks, meandered down the canyon floor. Willow grew in abundance and grasses were thick. They crossed and re-crossed the stream riding up the obvious trail. There was no attempt to brush out the prints. "Whoever that trailing rider was, he simply doesn't give two hoots whether he's being followed," Lamb chuckled.

"More than one ranch brings their cattle through here for grazing. Probably a line camp up further. Must be an outlet, too, cuz if I was runnin' from a posse I wouldn't come into a closed-up canyon." Oxford pointed up at a cathedral or rocks. "Good place for a man with a rifle, Lamb. Keep your eyes open."

They could see where the canyon turned to the south about half a mile in, and Buford called for a halt. "We better check that out on foot, Jake." They walked their horses to a stand of willow and tied off. Buford was looking up the side of the canyon to an outcropping that might give them a look into where the canyon turned. At this point, the canyon floor was about half a mile wide, and the sides were still steep. They could see the far ridges, several miles out and many feet higher.

It was a steep climb through tumbled rocks, thick sage, and loose ground, and took the young men half an hour to get to a perch where they could look down on the canyon floor. "Well, looky there," Jake Oxford said. "A cabin, corral, and three good looking horses, slightly lathered."

"We need to get the sheriff and Lester up here, Jake. You have the strongest horse, ride like the devil himself is chasing you and bring the sheriff. I'll keep watch and won't give our position away."

Oxford tried to be cautious slip-sliding back down the side of the mountain to the horses and rode off to bring the sheriff. Buford Lamb slowly worked his way down the other side of that ridge to get close enough to be in rifle range if the outlaws attempted to run. The cabin sat inside a stand of cottonwood trees, and there was about a hundred feet or so of open ground between the canyon

rocks and the trees. "Better just sit here and watch," Lamb
muttered.

The afternoon was blazing hot as Buford Lamb sat in
the rocks contemplating his situation. Three bank robbers
in that cabin and him, alone, but with a rifle and handgun.
*This is when everything Frank Acord talks about comes into play.
I know I've got back upcoming, but what would I do if they
weren't coming? What will I do if they don't?* Did he have
options? *My best bet, either way, is to sit here and wait 'em out.
They don't know I'm here, and that's my advantage. It's like that
ace in the hole in five-card stud.*

He could see the corral with three horses, plainly saw
how the canyon flared at this point, and the hills behind
the cabin weren't as steep as on his side. "They can't get to
their horses without me seeing them, but that sure would
be an easy run out of here," he muttered. "They got a good
thing goin' for 'em if the sweeper had done his job right.
Water, a cabin, probably well stocked. Always that one
mistake," he chuckled.

He thought it would be fun to goad the sweeper when
they put those boys in irons, watch him get all mad and
upset, maybe even do something dumb and get whupped
on. Buford Lamb had a nice smile as he settled in behind a
rock outcrop. *It's all right boys. I'll be here when you make your
move, whether the sheriff shows up or not.*

CHAPTER FOUR

"Get that trail wiped clean, did you?" Doolin demanded when Sandy Whiting barged into the cabin. Whiting was a skinny little man of about thirty years, had done time in Texas, he said, and in Mexico. Word was he had shot two men in the back in a fight near El Paso. He lied about anything and everything, regardless of the situation, and took great pleasure in working one man against another, just to see what happens.

"Yeah," he said and threw his buckskin jacket across the back of a chair, pulled his sombrero off and wiped trail dust from his face. "Where's the whiskey?"

George Fountain walked across the wide room and pulled a bottle from a cupboard and put it on the table. The cabin, just one large room, had cabinets along one wall with a cookstove on the opposite wall. There only the one door and the only window was alongside the door. It was primarily used as a more than comfortable line camp for the buckaroos holding their cattle on summer range.

"That was a damn fool stunt, grabbing that woman, Whiting," Doolin said. "You're gonna bring every lawman within a hundred miles around down on us. Damn fool stunt."

"Got us out of town without a scratch, Brad. Gotta think of things like that," he said with some pride spread across his thin face. "Not a single shot was fired at us, and they got themselves all busy trying to get her out of the river instead of chasing us. Hope you're smart enough to see that, Brad."

The direct challenge was thrown out, and Brad Doolin pulled his revolver and aimed it right at Whiting's right eye. "There weren't nobody lookin' to chase us, ya dumb bastard. I ought to pull the trigger, but we need your gun, Whiting. Don't be stupid again, cuz all you'll do is get us all killed. Now, we gotta get a plan put together, get out of this canyon alive, and make it east to the Reese River Canyon." He lowered the big revolver and slipped It into its leather, and Sandy Whiting leaped from his chair, slamming Doolin in the face with his mug full of whiskey.

Doolin, half blind from the whiskey grabbed the skinny little man and flung him across the small cabin's main room. Doolin had at least fifty pounds on the skinny Whiting who crashed into the rock wall and slowly sank to the floor, moaning. Doolin took three steps and drove his boot into Whiting's ribs bringing a sob from the little man. "When we get out of here you're on your own, Whiting. You're through. Look at me sideways between now and then and you'll be dead."

Whiting started to say something as Doolin turned back to the table and he spun around, planting a boot in Sandy Whiting's face. Doolin walked to the table and poured a cup full of whiskey and drank it down. His eyes stung, and he smelled like a saloon, but first things first, he said, "Let's count the money, George, before I go completely blind." He was wiping his eyes and growling out the words.

"I think we ought to leave right now, Brad. We could be on the river in several hours, get on the main road, and there wouldn't be any tracks to follow."

"Leave Sandy?"

"If he can't ride out now, he wouldn't be able to ride out tomorrow. What's the difference?" Fountain said. "We need him, and maybe that thrashing you gave him will do some good. Let's divvy the money, throw some grub in the saddle bags and get on the road."

"Okay, George, that's good. I'll count this stuff out, see if you can get that fool up and ready to ride, but if he can't, so be it."

Sheriff Acord and his deputy Lester Thompson were following Buford's trail with ease when Acord saw the dust of a rider coming toward them fast. "Hope that's Oxford or Lamb," he said. "Hope they found something."

Oxford pulled his pony up hard, yelling, "We found 'em, Sheriff. They got a cabin back in a deep canyon, and Buford's keepin' watch on 'em. We got 'em."

"Well, Mr. Oxford, we know where they are. Now it's time for us to get 'em," Acord chuckled. "Good work. Follow our trail, Thompson, and Jake, let's you and me high tail it back there. Lay it out for me on the way."

They were riding hard back toward the canyon, and Thompson described the little meadow in the canyon they found, with a cabin, cottonwood trees, and water. "Sounds like they could hole up for a while there," the sheriff muttered. "That cabin got solid walls, Jake?"

"Rock walls, Sheriff, and just one window that I could

see. Don't know if there was a back door. Corral was off to
the left, and the trail led off from behind the cabin. Not a
steep trail, either," Jake said. "It went right over the top,
probably out onto one of the high plains around here."

"Sounds good for their defense," Sheriff Acord said.
"Let's hurry. Several hours of daylight left and we might
just get lucky." They were riding hard through sage and
rabbitbrush with a few stands of cedar bushes and stunted
piñon pine, had to slow some negotiating their way
through drainage ditches and deeper arroyos, and made
good time getting to the canyon. They were covered in
sweat as were their horses. "Hotter than hades fires today,
Jake. Let's ride nice and slow; let these ponies cool out
some."

Buford Lamb, nestled in the rocks well above the
cabin, heard the ruckus inside even from his distant perch.
It was a hot summer afternoon, no breeze to ease the
waiting game, and Lamb wondered if he should make some
kind of play or wait and hope Sheriff Acord reached him
soon.

Lamb never got the chance to make a decision as he
watched the door of the cabin open and Doolin and Fountain walk out, carrying heavy saddle bags, bedrolls, and
canvas sacks full of gold and silver coins, and bills. He
pulled his rifle to his shoulder and made mistake number
one. He should have shot first and spoke later.

"Stop right there, Doolin. This is Deputy Sheriff
Buford Lamb. You're under arrest." Doolin dropped everything, spun away from the cabin pulling his revolver as he
fell to the ground. Fountain did the same, and the two
fired almost at the same moment as Lamb fired. Fountain
was hit in the chest with the rifle shot, but Doolin was not
hit and scrambled for the corral.

Lamb leaped to his feet, raced down out of the rocks and raised the rifle for an easy shot when a rifle barked out the cabin door, driving the deputy to the ground, the bullet hole dead center on his chest. Whiting crawled out of the doorway holding the rifle. "Better plan on helping me, Doolin. We need each other, now."

Doolin quickly saddled all three horses and used Fountain's for packing, tying everything helter-skelter to the saddle. He eased Whiting into his saddle, mounted, and they rode east on the trail that led out behind the cabin. "My ribs are gonna hurt for a long time, Doolin, so don't give me an excuse to shoot you. We ain't a team no more. We're just riding together for protection and don't forget it."

The words from the wounded man were empty as far as Doolin was concerned. They wouldn't be running if it weren't for Whiting's stupid move back in Winnemucca. He held himself in check but wanted to pull that big Colt and put an end to the bad man.

"That deputy was there because of your stupidity, Whiting. No, I won't forget it, won't forget that a good friend is dead because of it, that we're runnin' for our lives because of it. When we get to the main Emigrant Road, we'll split the money, and you can go your way. Look at me sideways, and I'll draw and quarter your butt."

Doolin and Whiting rode in silence as the late afternoon and evening began to come on fast. Midsummer evenings sometimes last well past the nine o'clock hour, and both were exhausted from hard riding since the robbery early that morning. Doolin pulled his horse up, and Whiting did the same. "Money's equally split in those two canvas sacks, Sandy. Pick the one you want and ride off. We're about ten miles from the main road."

Whiting had been trailing the pack horse, untied one of the sacks, and tied it to his saddle horn. "If we ever meet up again, Doolin, I'll kill you on sight." Doolin could see the pain in Whiting's eyes, watched as he rode off, doing what he could to not fall out of the saddle.

"Don't you fret none about that, Sandy Whiting," Doolin murmured. He took a turn on the pack horse's lead rope and glared at the outlaw. "I'll always see a snake like you first." He immediately forgot all about Whiting and Fountain and put his mind to saving himself. *If there was one deputy following us, there would be more coming to back him up, which means that I've got a posse riding down on me right now.* He let Whiting get well ahead of him then followed along as if they were riding together.

As the trail dipped through a gully that was still running with the remains of the last thunderstorm, he turned into the water and rode along the rocky bottom of the gully for the next three hours, leading the pack horse at a comfortable walk. It was so dark he had to stop before hurting himself or his horses. Riding up at the next easy spot, he saw some trees off in the distance and rode to them for a cold camp.

"I probably should have shot that snake. Whoever is following won't be put off by my little trick in the gully for very long. Gotta make Battle Mountain and find some help." He settled back on a downed cottonwood limb with half a smile on his bearded face. "Got seven thousand dollars in that bag there, so I just need to stay hid till thing quiet down."

He loved to rob stagecoaches and banks because of the ready cash, which he used to purchase the benefits of the working girls in the saloons across the great Nevada desert. He never got his full measure of a woman. There was no such thing as enough. Those thousands of dollars would vanish in clouds of vile conduct, and he'd be searching for another bank or stagecoach.

"How much further, Jake? This canyon seems to stretch out there for miles." Frank Acord spent more time behind his desk than he did in the saddle and today's ride was taking its toll.

"Canyon makes a big turn about half a mile up now, and that cabin sits in a little glade with trees and a freshwater spring. Buford is on a sidehill watching the cabin. He'll have his horse tied off where we can see it."

The two lawmen rode up to Lamb's horse, tied theirs off, and started climbing up the ridge to where they would meet with Buford Lamb. "Steep country," Acord said, stopping to catch his breath. "You say the cabin is just on the other side of this ridge? They picked a good place for a hideout. Wonder just how long they've been using it?"

"It's a line camp, Sheriff, and a good one. Buckaroo can keep close tabs on his herd and sleep warm at night. Good water right there, too," Oxford laughed.

They topped the ridge and ducked behind a stand of cedar to get a good look down at the cabin. "No horses and the door's open," Acord said. "Where's Lamb?"

"I see him, Sheriff. In those rocks down there." He was pointing at Lamb's body stretched out in the rocks and dirt, his rifle by his side. "Looks like he tried to stop their escape. There's another body in the corral."

Acord sent Oxford back for the horses and made his way down from the ridge to where Buford Lamb's body was laid out in the sun. "Damn fine man. Gonna miss you, boy," he said, kneeling down to make sure he was gone.

Acord checked on the body in the corral and then checked the cabin to make sure it was empty.

He was near the rear of the cabin when Jake Oxford rode up with their horses. "Three horses rode off that way," Acord pointed. "That trail should connect with the Emigrant road some miles out They'll be in Lander County before long if I know anything about Brad Doolin. That's his kind of country."

"Yeah, he's worked Lander, Eureka, White Pine counties for a couple of years now," Oxford said. "What's your plan, Sheriff?"

CHAPTER FIVE

Acord felt squeezed by what was happening. His force was here and were needed to continue the chase, and he felt he needed to be back in Winnemucca, to alert Lander County Sheriff Giles Murphy that Dolin might be headed his way. There would be many to question how he handled the situation.

"I'm going to give you what food is in my saddle bags, Jake, and I want you to trail these outlaws. I've got to get back to Winnemucca and get on the wires. Those lawmen in Lander and Eureka need to know that Doolin is coming their way.

"Do you want Lester to come on and follow you? No, that wouldn't work. We'll need that pack mule to get Buford's body back to town. I don't want to leave him out here."

"I'll be fine with what food I have and yours. Lester has plenty for you two. Let's get me packed, and I'll be off."

"Those men are killers, Jake, don't ever forget that. They know they are being followed, and that means they might set up traps to lead you into their guns. I'll let

Murphy know you're following. You're young, Jake, and you haven't had much experience with outlaws, so use that head of yours. Think about what it is you have to do."

"You taught me well, Sheriff. I might be young, but I'm also smart. I'll find those yahoos and bring 'em in," he said, a broad smile across his young face. Acord felt great sadness at the loss of Buford Lamb and felt secure knowing that Oxford would continue the chase.

Other lawmen, hearing about this felt, Acord was wrong. He should have sent the older man back with the mules to send out the wires and been the leader he was elected to be. Many felt he should have ridden with Jake Oxford.

Jake left out at a fast trot on a strong horse, and Acord waited for Lester Thompson. They wrapped the two bodies in blankets and tied them off on the mule and started the long ride back to town. "Gonna miss that boy," Acord said again. "Best damn deputy I ever had working for me, Lester."

"Jake gonna be okay out there by himself? He's a fine, strong young man, but that Doolin's a killer. Don't you think you should be riding with him?"

"He'll be fine, Lester. Just fine."

"According to this wire, Brad Doolin's bunch robbed the bank in Winnemucca, injured an old lady, and killed a deputy chasing him." Giles Murphy was a grizzled old lawman with the personality of an angry badger. He preferred killing over arresting, considered most judges simpletons or weak hearted, and drank his whiskey neat.

"Says Doolin is probably coming back this way. He's been active in the past along the Reese River," Murphy chuckled. "Or so the legend goes. His mama was a working girl making her money off the railroad boys. Never knew who his pa might be. Been worthless since the day she dropped him." He picked up the wire and read it again.

"Well, it's a good story, Murphy, but for real, Doolin came to us from the east. Just another outlaw comin' west." Shorty Evans chuckled. "These damn reporters just love to make things up about outlaws. Try to make 'em into Robin Hood or something."

Evans was an older man, set in his ways, and those included sitting in front of a pot belly stove with his feet up and fresh coffee in hand. He worked just hard enough to be able to tell himself he had worked, was not necessarily proud of wearing a badge; being a deputy was just a means of supporting himself. Shorty Evans was a slob, according to his friends.

"Frank Acord isn't leading the posse, in fact, there isn't a posse," Murphy growled. "That damn weak old man. Has just one young deputy following Doolin. Sumbitch of a stupid damn move." He scratched out a message on a piece of paper and handed it to Evans. "Send this up to Pete Simpson in Battle Mountain." Pete Simpson was the resident deputy in Battle Mountain. "He'll put together a posse and meet that Doolin head-on."

Murphy's Lander County Sheriff's Office was in the county courthouse in Austin, Nevada and Battle Mountain was at the far north end of the county, along the Emigrant Road and the Humboldt River. "When you get back, you'll be in charge. I'm leaving now for Battle Mountain. Send that same message to Ed Connors in Eureka County, too. Damn that Doolin.

"Well, he's a dead man if he comes into my county. Get those messages out and get right back here," Murphy said.

He had his heavy coat, a rifle, shotgun, and packed saddle bags in hand as he rambled out the door. "Don't dawdle and don't spend the afternoon at the saloon."

"What's that coat for, Sheriff? It's mid-summer."

The sheriff chuckled some, calling back over his shoulder. "That's my bedroll."

He rode down out of the Lander County seat into the Reese River Valley and turned north, following the Reese toward Battle Mountain. The Nevada Central Railroad tracks made the trip easier, and with the Reese River right there, the sheriff knew he would have fresh water all along the journey.

"Coulda waited for the train, I guess, but I like ridin' cross country. Besides, sure as hell, I'd have to talk to somebody on the trip." Conversations were usually one worded with Giles Murphy.

It was already late in the day when he started, so he rode until dark and made a simple cold camp near some cottonwood trees. There were ranches along the Reese River canyon, and Murphy would have been welcomed at any of them, but he also knew that a stop like that would have entailed hours of wasted time in talking about nothing. "Damn women would have fed me too much, damn men would have forced me to drink too much, and Doolin still wouldn't be caught," he grumbled, crawling under his heavy coat for the night.

A fast cup of coffee-soaked venison jerky with a cold biscuit, and he was in the saddle before the sun lightened the day. Coming out of the canyon put Murphy on a wide plateau that rose and fell; undulated ground he called it, with few highlights to guide him north. He simply followed the railroad tracks into town.

"Simpson left last night to head off Doolin and his

gang," Deputy Freddy Arnold told Murphy when the sheriff arrived.

"He ain't got no gang," Murphy snarled. "Fountain's dead and he's only got that weasel, Sandy Whiting. Get out on the street and do some patrolling, you don't need to be in the office. I'm going to the stables and get a shoe fixed on my horse then I'm riding out to meet with Simpson."

Arnold was used to a laid-back Pete Simpson approach to peacekeeping and jumped from the chair and hightailed it out onto the main street. Murphy had a hint of a smile as he made his way across to the stables and the blacksmith shop. "Another ten minutes? Damn, well, okay, I'll be next door, come get me when that horse is ready," he said. He grabbed the shotgun from the saddle, walked back onto the street, and turned into the Lucky Club for a cold beer. He took the shotgun from a stagecoach messenger in a poker game some time ago. It was a sawed-off double-barreled job in ten gauge, and Murphy cherished it like a favorite son.

"Gimme a cold one, Walter, and better back it up with some good whiskey."

"Comin' up, Sheriff," Walt Winters said. "Fresh barrel just come in." He didn't say whether the barrel was full of whiskey or beer

Murphy looked around the seedy little saloon. The bar was only five stools long, there was a faro table in the back, unused for gambling, but there were two men sitting there. There hadn't been a faro dealer in town for months. In fact, it was Winters who shot the previous one when he was caught cheating.

Besides the filthy window up front, the only light in the saloon came from equally filthy oil lamps hanging from the ceiling. Their pitiful attempt at brilliance was a failure, and it was only the daylight coming from the open double doors up front that gave any light to the room.

It took Murphy just half a second to recognize the skinny little man hunched over the faro table. "Damn me, but I am one lucky sumbitch today," he muttered. He took the whiskey down in one gulp, washed it some with beer and stepped toward the back of the narrow saloon. Sandy Whiting saw the bulky man walking toward him and went for his sidearm. He would have said his broken ribs slowed him down.

Murphy simply raised the shotgun and pulled both triggers. "So much for the Doolin gang," he murmured. Whiting was all but cut in half by the double blast of buckshot, and most of those in the bar were blinded by that same blast and the acrid black-powder smoke filling the room.

"Sorry for the mess, Walt, but this idiot robbed the Winnemucca bank and killed a Humboldt deputy yesterday. He is what's left of the Brad Doolin gang." Murphy looked at the man who had been sitting with Whiting.

"Who are you and what kind of business did you have with this backstabbing weasel?"

"He was asking me about roads in the area. Never seen him before, Sheriff. Honest. He ain't never been here before, he said. He said a horse threw him and busted his ribs."

"You better not be lyin' to me," Murphy growled. He finished reloading the menacing shotgun and told Walt to get some help cleaning up the mess. "Time to put Doolin in a grave real soon. Find my deputy, Mr. Simpson, and have him go through all Whiting's belongings. Probably carrying some of the Humboldt Bank money with him."

. . .

Jake Oxford had no trouble following the trail left by Whiting and Doolin, but as night came on, he knew he could lose it easily. He found a stand of cedar bushes and made camp. "Better to not lose them in the dark," he muttered. He was back on the trail at first light. "No one's been on this road since the three of them, so trailin' them ain't hard."

It was an hour later that he realized he was trailing only one horse and turned back to find out where the two others dropped off. He found three horses had ridden into a ditch with running water in it, but only one horse rode out. "Clever," he said and had to make a decision on which trail to follow.

"They must have split the money and then gone separate ways," he muttered. "So, Jake Oxford, what would Sheriff Acord do?" He muttered and mumbled to himself for a full five minutes and finally decided that it would be far easier to follow the man on the main trail. "I can stay with him and at least know where the other two went," he decided, riding up and out of the ravine.

He could see Battle Mountain about five miles off and also saw a rider approaching at a fast trot, about half a mile off. He rode slowly and pulled up when the rider reached him. "Who are you?" Sheriff Giles Murphy demanded.

"Humboldt County Deputy Jake Oxford," Jake said. Oxford had met Murphy on one occasion and remembered how much the man frightened him. "I'm trailing one of the men that robbed the bank in Winnemucca and killed our deputy, Buford Lamb. Did you pass someone riding out, Sheriff?"

"Yeah," Murphy said, thinking hard. "Sandy Whiting's

dead, but where is Doolin? How about you? You should have run into my deputy, Pete Simpson."

"Haven't seen anyone this morning 'ceptin' you. I think I know where he is, though," Oxford said. He spent the next few minutes telling about how the trail seemed to lead up the ravine that had water running in it. "There were three horses rode into the gulch, and one rode out," he said. "Your deputy probably got there before me this morning and is following that little creek."

"You're riding with me, boy. Let's follow that creek and see what we find."

CHAPTER SIX

It was a cold morning when Brad Doolin pulled the blanket off. It was the middle of August, but in the high mountain deserts of Nevada, Doolin knew he would be facing a very hot ride as the day wore on. He made a small fire, had some coffee and biscuits, and loaded his pack. *That weasel Whiting will be in Battle Mountain and sure as hell will stir something up. Gonna have to be careful.* His mind was full of problems, and his thoughts became words.

"I'll skirt town and head up the Reese River to Austin. Hopefully, they'll concentrate on Whiting and not my trail. Now I gotta fight a big posse because of a dead deputy shot by Whiting. Shoot the banker, that's okay. Don't shoot the lawman." Doolin seemed to forget that Buford Lamb was about to shoot him when Whiting fired.

It was rough country, and there were enough people in that country that he had to be careful to not catch someone's attention. He was well away from the drainage ravine and working his way toward the Central Pacific Railroad line. He could follow those tracks toward Battle Mountain and then swing south into the Reese country. There was only game trails where he was, a few scattered ranches, and he spent most of the day simply working his way cross-country, constantly looking behind him for signs of a posse.

He had no trouble staying far from what few ranches there were, didn't run into any ranchers out tending cattle, and kept a close eye on what might be going on behind him. The sky was an endless blue, sporadically dotted with puffy white clouds, and what wind there was helped cool him off.

Pete Simpson followed that ravine for several miles keeping close watch on the sides, and it wasn't hard for him to find where Doolin left the ravine. Just a few miles further and he found the still warm camp where Doolin spent the night. "I gotcha, boy," Simpson muttered, kicking his horse into a nice trot.

Doolin was still trailing Fountain's horse and after a couple of hours knew he had to let it go. The cross-country riding was hard enough, and he needed all the speed he could get. "I gotta get to that river bottom just as soon as I can." He moved essentials from the pack horse to his saddle bags, pulled the tack from the horse and turned it loose. He was now able to ride at a fast trot and made for the Humboldt River and the railroad.

Simpson was a laid-back, busted up ex buckaroo who found the life of a resident deputy to his liking. Bust a drunk across the side of the head once in a while, break up a fight with the butt of your rifle now and then, and flirt with all the ladies of the town was to his liking. Getting out like this and riding your horse cross country reminded him of wonderful days of moving cattle through rugged Nevada mountains and valleys.

Riding long circles from sunup to sundown, moving cattle out of high country in the fall, moving them into the mountains in the spring. He missed those days, missed the camaraderie of his fellow buckaroos, but surely didn't miss some of the horrible food that was served. "We made a drive south one year, it was a four-day drive, and I swear they didn't have one single thing that could be called food on that chuck wagon," he laughed. "Well, come on; let's get us a killer."

Life was good for Simpson, but he didn't have enough knowledge of what it meant to chase a dangerous outlaw, a man who had just robbed a bank and killed a deputy sheriff. He was riding through brush and rocks and the closer he got to the Humboldt River, the thicker the brush became, and more stands of trees he had to negotiate through, and the less time he spent keeping his eye on what was out in front of him.

Doolin's heading for the Humboldt River and I'd be willing to bet he's gonna turn east to find the Reese River and head south. Lots of country to hide in that way. Simpson had it figured right, but the idea of Doolin setting up an ambush never entered his mind.

He rode over a rise in the desert and found the saddle and bridle from the pack horse, the old horse standing off to the side munching on some grass. "So, it isn't two men I'm following," Simpson said. "Just one, eh? He's looking to make good time, and I'm gonna chase him down."

It was Doolin who was keeping his eyes open, front and back. Doolin had spent the greatest part of his life running from something, his mother, ugly men he robbed or beat up, and the law. He spotted Simpson's dust and knew it wasn't just somebody out for a long ride in the desert.

There was a tumble of rocks near a spring surrounded by cottonwood trees, and Doolin rode to the springs. He tied his horse off in good grass, grabbed his rifle and ran for the rocks, about fifty yards or so away. "That fool will ride to my horse, and I'll drop him before he realizes what he's done wrong," Doolin laughed. He tucked in behind some boulders and half an hour later watched Simpson ride slowly toward the trees.

He had the sun behind him, his horse was standing in good grass in the shadows, and he took one last check to make sure that Winchester had one in the chamber.

"Just another little bit, mister," Doolin said sighting the rifle on Simpson's chest. Simpson rode right up to the tied off the horse and stepped out of the saddle. He ducked down to adjust his pants leg just as Doolin pulled the trigger, and the bullet slammed into the horse's side, dropping him.

Simpson hit the ground, snaked his way through high grass and rocks to a downed cottonwood and heard a second bullet scream over his head. He hadn't grabbed his rifle and pulled a Colt from its leather, looking around for a better place to be. "Don't know where that fool is? Gotta get somewhere I can shoot." He wanted to look over the top of the rocks he was behind but knew better.

Doolin cussed a storm for a few seconds when he missed with the second shot and decided it would be best to slow himself down, pay attention to the shot, and be back on the trail. He knew where Simpson was and knew the man didn't know where he was. "Just stay calm and still, Brad Doolin and you'll get your shot."

Simpson saw a little depression in the ground that led

to a stand of trees interspersed with some large rocks. It would be at least five yards of open space, and he tensed, leaped and rolled toward that depression. Doolin was ready, aimed and fired, levered another round into the chamber and fired again.

Simpson was hit with both rounds. The first tore through his shoulder from the top down deep into his chest. The second shot, not necessary, entered the top of his head and came out along his neck.

"So you're somebody's deputy, eh?" He was standing over Simpson's body looking at the big tin star on his vest. "Well, not much of one now," Doolin said, taking the man's rifle from its scabbard and mounting his horse. "So long, sucker. I got me bags of gold, and there be women waiting for me," he laughed. *I wonder why there is just one deputy following me? Shouldn't there be a whole posse? Hell, we robbed a bank, threw an old lady in the river, and killed another deputy. Just one deputy, and now he's dead. This might be the best day of my life. They won't know he's dead for days.*

"How long you been riding for Acord?" Giles Murphy never did get along with Frank Acord. Acord figured the sheriff's job was to see to it that his deputies kept the peace. Murphy figured his job was to kill outlaws thereby keeping the peace. "Why'd he send you out alone?"

"Frank had me, old man Lester Thompson, and Buford Lamb chasing Doolin's gang from the bank, but Acord held back with Lester and me, and Lamb found Doolin's hideout. I rode back to bring the sheriff, but Doolin killed Lamb before we got back. Lamb did kill George Fountain before he got shot.

"Acord rode back to alert you and Ed Connors."

"Damn fool. Should have sent the old man back. Well, my deputy, Simpson is following Doolin right now, and we gotta catch up. I killed Whiting in town before I left, so it's Doolin we're following. He's a dangerous man, Jake. Don't ever forget that. Plan him being behind every rock we see, behind every tree, ready to kill every second of every day."

They were several hours behind Simpson, and it was late in the day when they rode up on the saddle and bridle in the desert. The old horse was still standing nearby, munching grass. "These prints are old, Sheriff," Jake said. "Look how the wind has knocked them down. We're a long way behind."

They had no trouble following the trail Doolin and Simpson left. The only other prints they saw were from other types of animals. The horse prints stood out. "It's one on one, with Doolin having the upper hand, Oxford. Simpson's a good resident deputy but he ain't no tracker. We gotta catch up. He'll ride into an ambush sure as I'm sittin' here." Murphy spurred his horse into a long and fast trot that eats miles, and they rode into the gathering evening.

"There's a nice spring about five miles in front of us, Oxford. We'll camp up there. Gonna be damn dark soon. When we spot those trees, we ride slow, and we split up. I'll take the high side in; you ride in with your eyes and ears wide open, you hear me?" Murphy knew those springs and knew they would offer a perfect ambush site.

"I gotcha, Sheriff," Jake said.

Murphy looked back at the young deputy, saw a set to his mouth and eyes, a hardness that comes from under-standing yourself despite your youth, and smiled. *Frank Acord doesn't know the gem he has wearing that badge. Might just ask this boy to go to work for me.* He chuckled, putting the spurs to his horse.

As they approached the springs in the failing light, Murphy pulled off to ride in through the jumbled rocks of the hillside and Jake rode toward the cottonwoods. Oxford spotted the downed horse and pulled up a hundred yards or so away, stepped off his horse and grabbed his rifle for a slow approach.

When he was about twenty-five yards out, he spotted the body sprawled in the dirt. "Got a body and a dead horse, Sheriff," he yelled out.

"Comin' in," Giles Murphy yelled back, bounding down out of the rocks. "Damn, Mr. Simpson. Gonna miss you, old man." Murphy spent less than ten minutes checking out the area, working out what his next move should be.

"Let's get Mr. Simpson buried, protected from the animals. His family can come and reclaim the body later, and then we gotta move fast for town. Doolin knows the Reese River from the Humboldt to the Toyabe Mountains, and I gotta get a posse organized."

Jake Oxford was young, had been a deputy for just a year, and was having a hard time holding on. First, he found the body of his best friend and fellow deputy and now, he walked up to the body of another deputy. Both men killed by Brad Doolin in his mind. "I want to ride with you on that posse, Sheriff," he said. The grave was shallow, and he piled dirt and rocks over the dead Pete Simpson.

"Acord won't like it, but it's okay with me," Murphy growled. "We get back, I gotta send wires to Austin and then to Eureka. If we put pressure on Doolin, we can keep him moving, and it'll be easier to nail him hard and fast.

Don't want to give him time to find a hidey hole which I've heard he's good at."

He paced around and finally said, "We can't ride cross country with no moon, Oxford. We'll make camp and ride out at first light."

CHAPTER SEVEN

Giles Murphy, Freddy Arnold, and Jake Oxford rode out of Battle Mountain late the following day, with no visible trail to follow. The road south to Austin was a busy one despite the fact that the railroad covered the same ground. Ranches and mines were scattered all along the way, travel between the two main towns in Lander County was regular, and a single rider wouldn't particularly stand out.

"All we can hope for is someone recognizing him," Murphy said. The only men in town were too old to ride or too young. Buckaroos were busy at the scattered ranches, and the mines were hiring anyone with a pulse. "We all know what Doolin looks like and he is known along this road, so we might get lucky."

If it weren't for the mission they were on, Jake Oxford was thinking, this would be a beautiful ride. The Reese River should be called the Reese Creek at best, but it flowed this summer day, through rich farm and ranch country. Each of the little farms along the creek had fruit trees and gardens lush with fruit and vegetables, and the cattle and sheep they saw were fat.

Murphy had a plan of sorts and knew it was full of holes since Doolin had such a good jump on them. "Two of my deputies in Austin will ride down out of town to the valley after making sure Doolin hasn't already come through town and hopefully cut him off."

"Can he get east without going through Austin?" Oxford had never been to that silver rich little town, didn't know that it was perched on the side of a hill and that there were several canyons that threaded through the towering Toyabe Range. "What happens if he goes south?"

"Yeah, he can and no he won't," Murphy snarled. "He's made enemies with the Yomba Indians and if he goes south, they'll either kill him or give him up." He chuckled, "Or eat him. I'm betting he'll make a run around Austin and a hard ride through the mountains."

It was a long ride through the canyon to the Reese River Valley, and despite stopping a few people and asking about Doolin, asking at a couple of the ranches, they still didn't know if Doolin had actually come that way. "Gettin' dark fast. Let's set up camp in those trees and get back on it first light," Murphy said.

They were in the process of getting organized when Aaron Snider and Shorty Evans, the deputies from Austin, rode in fast. "Got trouble, Sheriff," Evans yelled out. "At the Hanley Ranch."

"Doolin?" Murphy yelled.

"Old man Hanley and his wife are dead and their boy, Spider, barely alive, said it was Doolin. He's heading east, Giles."

"To hell with camp, we're riding in the dark for Austin," Murphy said. Everyone scrambled to get saddled for the ride. They still had well over twenty miles to go.

"Don't be plannin' on much sleep when we get there. I want us on the road at first light."

They were on a regular roadway, not cross country, so there was little danger in riding hard in the dark. There was just enough starlight to keep them on the pathway. They rode out of the canyon and into the Reese River Valley, and now, faced a stiff climb to the little town of Austin. "I figure it's about three," Murphy said. "Be saddled, have a good pack with plenty of smoked or dried meat. We ain't taking a mule or pack horse. We leave at sunrise."

Oxford opted to take a cot in one of the cells as did Aaron Snider. Shorty Evans went home to his wife, and Giles Murphy got old man Smith at the cafe up to put together packages of meat and biscuits, bags of coffee beans, and bags of dried beans. "Don't know how long we'll be gone, Smitty, so just make enough for three days, and we'll fend for ourselves after that."

"Shorty said the Hanley's were dead. That right?"

"Yup. We'll catch the bastard, though. He killed Pete Simpson, too, along with a Humboldt County deputy. He's a mean, one, old man, but so am I." Murphy almost smiled, saying that. Murphy sent Arnold back to Battle Mountain. "I know you want to ride with us, but those people in Battle Mountain need you, too."

They rode to the Hanley ranch, deep in a canyon east of Austin and circled around twice before finding Doolin's trail out. "He'll circle around these hills for most of the day before dropping into the Big Smoky Valley. He's got no friends in that valley, but he does have in Eureka and further east." Everyone took a close look at the prints left by Doolin, hoping they would be able to identify them in the event he moved onto a main road.

"He's staying off the main trail, Sheriff," Shorty Evans said. "Hope he don't stay off it. Sure will make trackin' him easier." Evans was the oldest of the men, wasn't the brightest, but was strong, a good shot, and did what he was told.

"You got that all backwards, Shorty. If he gets on the main road, his tracks will get all messed up with other riders. If he stays cross-country like this, he's easier to track. You just lookin' for the easy ridin'. You ain't gettin' it on this chase." Shorty Evans just looked away and chuffed a bit.

It was mid-morning by the time they were actually out searching. "I sent wires to Belmont, Eureka, and Ely, so half the state will be looking for the fool," Murphy said.

Doolin knew he wouldn't be spotted on the road from Battle Mountain to Austin, but also knew that Sheriff Murphy would have people in Austin waiting for him. He figured on riding around Austin, and heading east, around Eureka, and getting into the mountains south of Ely. There were several mining areas where he could hide out, and there were good pickin's as far as gold shipments went. He needed to sleep and a small pack of food.

He circled around south of Austin and up through the foothills and dropped into a deep canyon on the east side of town. He boldly rode up to Fred Hanley's ranch, tied off his horse and pounded on the kitchen door. Evaline Hanley opened the door, and before she could even say hello, Doolin shot her dead, pushed her body out of the way, and strode into the kitchen, just as old man Hanley and his ten-year-old boy came running.

"What the..." is as far as the rancher got. Doolin shot Hanley through the chest and shot the boy high on his shoulder, driving him clear out of the kitchen. Doolin didn't bother checking any of the bodies; what he was there for was food. He ransacked the cupboards and barrels, filled sacks, and walked out to his horse. Two old ranch hands stood on the bunkhouse porch, wiping sleep from their eyes, as he rode off the ranch and into the canyon. The old men were the nighthawks, who rode to keep wolves, mountain lions, and rustlers away from the small Hanley herd and were awakened by the gunfire. The buckaroos were out on the range, and Doolin just rode off.

Doolin had hunted that canyon and nearby mountain-sides many times, knew the lay of the land well and made good time through rough timber, vertical canyon walls, and deep streams. The day was pleasant through the high mountains. Austin sits at six-thousand feet above sea level, and this canyon he was riding through was well over seven thousand. It just kept going higher and higher. A slight breeze was blowing, and he and his horse stayed cool all day.

He could see massive thunderstorms brewing to his west and south, knew that he would be in for it later in the day and started looking for someplace to hunker down. Large stands of pine, fir, and cedar dotted the hillsides at this altitude, but if he kept climbing, he'd be above timber-line and open to the thunder and lightning attack. He needed to stay in the trees.

The Toyabe Range is majestic with peaks reaching over ten thousand feet. Those peaks were often covered in snow year 'round, and the range seemed to draw fierce thunderstorms its way. Summer storms filled the creeks to overflowing, fed the grasses, and flowed east to the Big Smoky Valley and west to the Reese River Valley.

He was nearing a steep climb out of the canyon as

night came on. "Come on, boy, we'll climb out of this canyon before we make camp. It'll be a long ride downhill come morning, and Eureka in three or four days." It got cold as soon as the sun went down and Doolin made his camp almost at the ridge top. There was plenty of pine and aspen wood for a fire, and he had some good fresh meat from the Hanley ranch for supper, along with apple pie and coffee.

He was settled in, tarps hung as a lean-to covered his bedroll, and a good fire kept him warm as the thunder shook the ground he was sitting on. Rain poured as if flowing from an upturned barrel, lightning split the skies, and he knew that if there were men following, they too would be bunkered in.

He hadn't had time to think about anything but getting away since the bank robbery in Winnemucca, and as he sat by the fire on this stormy summer evening, he knew he had to have a plan, or they would catch him sure as hell. Doolin didn't have a quick mind and found himself on a high ridge in a wilderness fraught with danger.

"Ward," he muttered. "That's where I need to get to. They got good mines with money flowing in and out and plenty of mountains to hide in. It'll take me a week to get there from here, hell ten days at least, and I'm gonna need a lot more food than I got." He threw a couple more chunks of wood on the fire, had another cup of coffee.

The thunderstorm ended as quickly as it began, and the night turned cold with thousands of stars shining on the wet forest. "I'd sure like to ride into Eureka and hit that bank. Those mines are cooking right now." His mumbling only lasted another few minutes, and he was under the blankets, sound asleep.

. . .

"This just came in, Sheriff. Looks important." Old man Whitby from the telegraph office was out of breath when he barged into the office. Ed Connors and Terrence Corcoran were jawin' over some hot coffee, and tellin' lies like they did most afternoons. "It's from Giles Murphy."

Connors read the long wire and handed it to Corcoran. "Time for you to go to work, old man. That idiot Brad Doolin's done it this time. When Giles asks for help, it must really be bad."

Corcoran took the note and read it quickly. "He says Doolin was being chased across the Toyabe range and into the Smoky Valley, and raided a ranch, killing the family there. He is probably headed for our country." Corcoran's jaw was hardened, and his eyes narrowed as he folded the wire and handed it back.

"You think he'll come here or go south to Belmont? He's got the bank money, remember." Ed Connors was getting his maps out and spreading them on the desk. "If he goes to Belmont, there ain't nothing south of there to draw him."

"No, he'll head right for us. Only three places, Belmont, Antelope Valley, and here. Ain't nothing in Belmont for him." Corcoran grabbed the big map the sheriff had and unrolled it. "He sure as hell isn't going to the Antelope Valley. The Duck Valley Shoshone Reservation is down that way.

"We have mines, a big bank, stagecoaches, and ranches for him to pick from. I'll put together a little pack and ride out and ambush that snake. He's killed his last lawman, Ed. There's two ranches about forty miles west, and I'd make a bet he'll hit one of 'em."

"You want Snell to ride with you?"

"No, you need him here. I wouldn't argue you riding

along, but if he gets around me, you need to be here, too. I'll go alone with a pack horse. Spread the word around town just in case he gets around me. He's mean, stupid as the day is long, but cagey. He don't give quarter to no one, just shoots and robs."

Corcoran knew that Ed Connors was a big, strong buckaroo, and knew the man had never worn a badge before this election. He would grow into the job, but Corcoran also knew that he would be the training officer for these first few months.

Corcoran walked across to the Bonanza Club and found Cindy Payton in the kitchen. She ran across and threw herself in his waiting arms. "Need some trail food, sweetheart," he said, nuzzling her neck. He set her down, patted her ample bottom, and gave her a gentle kiss.

"Where we goin?" She giggled and squirmed around, giving the big deputy ideas he didn't want to have at the moment.

"Just me, little one. Gonna find me a killer and make him sorry for letting me find him. Need about two or three days' worth that will go on a pack horse, so don't be skimpy." He gave her bottom another friendly pat and walked out to the bar.

"Doolin might be comin' this way, Jimmy," he said. "Goin' after that bastard, I am. Cindy's throwing a food bundle together for me. Mind slipping a bottle of good bourbon in the pack. Gotta get my horses put together."

Henderson laughed, saying he'd get right on it. "Bill the county, should I?"

"You bet," Corcoran yelled back from the batwing doors. He was on the trail in less than twenty minutes, and eyes were on him riding out of town.

. . .

"Where do you suppose he's goin?" Butch Clemons and Ed Reason were riding down off a side hill south of Eureka as Terrence Corcoran rode out of town leading a pack horse. "Suppose he's looking for them cattle?"

"We got 'em hid pretty good, Butch, but we better follow. That buyer from Elko is coming Tuesday, and we gotta get them new brands ironed in. This ain't the time for the the law to be snooping around."

Clemons and Reason had been raiding ranches in the area for months, slowly building their herd and making runnin' irons to create a brand they registered. Along with the rustled cattle they also were good at snatching unbranded calves out on the grass. They called 'em 'strays.' Gilbert Bentley, a buyer with few scruples, was coming to pick up the herd and get it shipped before too many people even knew Clemons and Reason had a herd.

Butch Clemons had been rustling cattle in Colorado and New Mexico Territory and had to run for his life when he picked up ten good head from the Territorial Governor and sold them back to him with his altered brand work. The re-burned brand was noticed, and Clemons had to run for his life. That run brought him to Nevada where he tied up with the small-time thief and hard-nosed Ed Reason in Elko. They moved into the cattle-rich Diamond Valley of Eureka County and began building their herd.

"If he gets anywhere near those pens, we gotta kill that man," Reason said. "Should anyway, I say."

"For the time being, let's just follow along." Clemons wore his hair longer than most, wore a massive mustache, and had a pointed goatee. He loved the ladies and knew they enjoyed the company of a cattleman. That was his entire purpose in rustling. To build a herd without having to buy the starter heifers or the land to put them on. "Corcoran's got a nose for trouble, and his guns are faster than anything I've ever seen."

Reason wanted to argue the point but didn't. "The railroad comes right up the valley and connects at the cattle pens. We got our cows about five miles out in that little boxed up canyon, and if Corcoran rides toward that, I'm gonna kill him, Butch. Bentley's offered us five dollars a head, and that's good money I ain't willing to lose."

"We'll play the hand as it's dealt, Ed," is all Clemons said.

The main road west dipped down into the valley within a mile of Eureka's main town, and the railroad had a station there for watering and wood, the ranchers had many cattle pens scattered around, and there were convenient track-side loading docks as well. "When Gil makes the deal, we'll move the cattle right up to those loading docks and get them in the cars before anyone even knows we've been there."

The rail line runs north with connection to the Intercontinental line. Cattle from most of the western ranches stay west of the Rocky Mountains with feedlots in most of the major towns. There are thousands of people looking for good beef from Salt Lake City to San Francisco.

CHAPTER EIGHT

"I'll make the Cornell ranch late today and see if anyone's seen or heard anything," Corcoran murmured. "Best place to jump Doolin will be at the Antelope Valley Road. He'll have to come through that pass, and he won't want to skirt around it." Like most people who spend countless hours alone, whether in the saddle or at a desk, Corcoran had great conversations with himself. "I'm a philosophizin' giant when I'm talking great ideas with Dude," he liked to quip.

He's been riding Dude for more than ten years after taking him from an old man who thought the best way to train a horse was using an ax handle. Dude didn't much care for men after getting trained for some time, but Terrence Corcoran had his way, and the two are inseparable.

He was known to talk to Dude, just as if he was a person. Corcoran had a long ride ahead of him and was laying out his plan as he rode. "I can get in those rocks south of the pass and see downhill east and west. Doolin ain't gettin' around us, Dude."

It was a beautiful summer day, hot, but a cooling breeze made the ride through open country enjoyable. "Probably get drenched this afternoon," he chuckled. Great columns of thunderheads were already building over the mountains to the west.

He passed the road that ran north through Diamond Valley, passed a couple of roads heading south toward active mines, and saw the dust from some buckaroos moving cattle toward the railhead. "Looks almost peaceful out there, don't it, Dude? Well, old friend, it ain't. Just look at us, chasing a killer, and might get him, too." The Cornell ranch was still some twenty miles off.

He made another five miles before he realized he was being followed. "Hanging back, are you?" He murmured. He was in rolling open plains and spotted a stand of cottonwood trees about a hundred yards off the trail when he rode over a slight rise. He kicked the horses into a trot and tucked into the trees, tying the animals in some grass. "Let's see who you are."

He grabbed his rifle and worked his way back toward the main road, keeping low through the sagebrush, rabbit-brush, and scrub cedar. He was well hidden as Clemons and Reason rode right on past him. He let them get ahead and quickly ran to his horses, mounted, and was following the outlaws within minutes.

"Now, we'll find out where you boys are going, eh?" He was chuckling, moving at a fast walk half a mile behind. "I've been wanting to know something about those two for some time. Maybe I'll learn something today."

"Wherever he's going, it ain't to where we got them cows tucked in," Butch Clemons said. "The trail to our canyon is back behind us a few miles. Let's check on them and call it a day. I could drink a barrel of beer right now."

"I guess you're right," Reason said. "Sure was looking forward to killin' that man."

They turned back toward town, and as they rode over a rise in the trail, they came face to face with Corcoran. "Howdy, boys. Out for a nice ride, are you? Got your picnic lunch and everything?" Corcoran had a grand smile plastered across his Irish mug. "It certainly is a nice day for a picnic."

"You followin' us?" Reason demanded.

"It's a public road, Mr. Reason. Some reason I should be followin' you, gentlemen? I heard there's a cattle buyer comin' to town in the next few days. You boys sellin' some?"

"Get out of the way, Corcoran," Reason snarled. He put the spurs to his horse, but Corcoran and his pack horse didn't move, and Reason had to pull up.

"Let's not get hasty, Reason. You got cattle to sell?"

"We've had a fair year, Corcoran," Butch Clemons said. "Our heifers dropped some pretty calves this year, and we're sellin' a few." Clemons needed to get Reason calmed down and get the two of them out of there. He knew how Corcoran could intimidate, knew Corcoran could provoke Reason into doing something stupid and knew Reason wasn't good enough to face that Irisher one on one.

"Heard there's a piece of land out this way and wanted to look it over." Clemons nudged his horse. "We're just riding back to town now." He wondered how Corcoran got behind them and was thankful they hadn't ridden up to that canyon.

Corcoran smiled at the bald-faced lie but didn't call Clemons on it. "Maybe I'll swing by the stockyards when the train comes in, meet that buyer of yours. Well, have a good day, gentlemen." Corcoran tipped the brim of his sombrero and nudged his horse forward. "Always be friendly with your neighbors but brand those calves," he laughed.

"He knows something," Reason said. "We need to kill him, Butch." Reason's hand was reaching for his rifle. "One shot in the back and our problems are over."

"Not a chance, Ed. Shoot a deputy in the back and say our problems are over?" *Man ain't got brain one. Every lawman in Nevada would be down on us. I made my biggest mistake letting him join up with me.* "Let's let him get well ahead of us and then follow some more. He's onto something, and I don't think it's us."

Corcoran was well aware of the two behind him when he rode into the Cornell ranch late that afternoon. "Afternoon, Johnny, how's things?" He said. He found John Cornell and two of his hands standing near the barn.

"Corcoran," Cornell yelled out. "Nice surprise this is. Addy and Marvell will be mighty surprised and glad to see you. Light yourself, my boy."

"Not completely a neighborly visit, John," Corcoran said, stepping off his horse. "There's danger about that we need to talk some about."

"Coffee's always on, Terrence. Come on in." John Cornell was originally from England but came to this country as a youngster. His folks came west at the first notices of gold being found in California and did well raising beef, fruit, and vegetables that they sold in a store in what was first called Hangtown and then, a little nicer, perhaps, Placerville. He moved to Nevada and established a successful ranch in Eureka County in the late 60s.

. . .

"That's quite a story, Corcoran," Cornell said. He walked to a cabinet and brought out a bottle of brandy. "I've heard of this Doolin character like most in these parts. What makes you think he's coming this way?"

"Nowhere else to go, Johnny. No reason to go south to Belmont, no reason go up and over into Antelope Valley. Shoshone have had too many white visitors to welcome an outlaw. He's caused so much trouble with the Indians they'll kill him on sight. He'll be looking to put a new gang together and move into country with banks, mines, and money moving around. That's his game, but he's on the run from murdering lawmen and women.

"Right now, Brad Doolin is the most dangerous man in Nevada, and your ranch is on his path. I would consider this man a mad fiend."

Addy Cornell and her daughter, Marvell walked in about that time. "Fiend? What kind of fiend are you bringing us, Terrence?" She laughed, sitting down at the table.

"Oh, he's not joking, mother," John said. "A bank robber and murderer might be comin' across the desert, and he's giving me a warning."

"My heavens," Marvell said. She stood just to Corcoran's left and put her hand on his shoulder. "That's awfully nice of you, Terrence," she said. Marvell had turned seventeen earlier in the spring and was making it very obvious that she'd certainly like to know this big, friendly deputy a lot better. "Will you be staying here to protect us?" She had big brown eyes, fluttered her lashes a bit, and smiled like an angel.

"No, Marvie, honey, I'll have to be out on the road to stop him." He slipped an arm around her thin waist and pulled her in close. "That way I can keep everyone safe," he laughed, and she moved toward the stove.

He nodded when the lovely Miss Cornell offered more coffee and nodded again toward the bottle of brandy. "Does make the coffee taste better." She smiled again, and he had to turn his eyes to John. "How many people you got here, John?"

"My hands are up in the mountains with the cattle, Terrence. Got just the two barn boys you saw out there, and my cook. My wife Addy and daughter Marvel are both excellent shots, Terrence, and my barn boys are too. We'll give him a hot time if he shows his face around this place."

"Make sure everyone is aware of the danger. I'm gonna move up to the ridge where the valley road cuts in and try to cut that fool off. He's probably only one day away." Marvell moved quickly to his side as he stood up and Terrence gave her a nice hug. "You help keep your mama and pa safe, Marvie. I'll be back to check on you."

"Where's he going now?" Reason and Clemons were tucked in behind a stand of trees and watched Corcoran ride out of the Cornell ranch and back on the main road. "Man's got a mission of some kind. Do you know Johnny Cornell?"

"Met him a time or two," Butch Clemons said. "Think he might have some calves for sale?" He had a sly smile on his face.

"Yeah, let's ride in and find out what Corcoran's up to."

They waited a full half hour before moving out from the trees and made their way to the Cornell ranch house. John Cornell was heading for the barn when they called to him. "Morning Mr. Cornell," Clemons said. "Don't know if you remember me. I'm Butch Clemons. We met at a cattleman's meeting one time."

"Don't believe I do, Mr. Clemons," Cornell said. He gave the dusty, unshaved man and his companion a close look. "What brings you out this way?" *They don't look like the man Corcoran described, but that skinny one is an outlaw if I've ever seen one. Should be carrying my shotgun, I think.*

"Lookin' to build our herd some and hoped you might have a young heifer or two for sale. We had a good crop of bull calves but not many heifers to hold back this spring."

"Got nothing for sale, men. Need everyone I have," Cornell said. "Might try some of the boys up the Diamond Valley."

"They be pretty stingy with theirs, too," Clemons chuckled. "Well, thanks." He started to turn his horse back. "Was that Deputy Sheriff Corcoran we saw riding off as we came down the trail?"

"Yeah, it was," Cornell said. "Looking for a mean killer might be riding this way. You boys might want to keep your eyes open as well."

Killer, eh?" Clemons looked over at Reason. "Thanks, Mr. Cornell. We sure will do that."

"Said it was Brad Doolin. Killed a couple of deputies, a rancher and his wife, and robbed a bank, too. He's a mean one. Ride safe, boys," Cornell said and walked into the barn. He smiled and nodded to the two barn-boys holding cocked rifles.

Clemons led Reason out to the main road. "I've heard of this Doolin, Reason. Let's follow behind Corcoran and see what happens."

"Might be a good time to kill that bastard," Reason said. "Make it look like that Doolin did it," he laughed right out. "Then we can kill Doolin and get the ree-ward."

The road west had been used by many thousands making their way to the California gold fields and later to the Comstock where silver by the pound waited. The land was rolling hills often featuring great outcrops of rock, small streams could be followed with the eye by the strands of green, willows lining the creeks, and natural springs were always fitted out with cottonwood trees.

Corcoran found a copse of cottonwood and willow, some cold-water bubbling from a spring and made camp. "Tomorrow will put me at the crossroads, and I'll wait for Mr. Doolin," he muttered. He had a small fire and ate good roast beef, drank from Jimmy Henderson's whiskey, and watched the stars move through the endless skies. "It's only the fact I'm chasing a killer that puts a dark tint to a night like this."

Morning chores done, Corcoran was on the trail. "Forty miles or so, Dude, and we'll set a trap for old Mr. Doolin. Have you ever seen so much open land? Not a house, not a herd of cattle or yowlin' buckaroos within ten thousand miles, it feels like. Hope it stays like this forever." Some of the surrounding mountains still had snow at their very peaks while the grasses in the valleys were starting to brown out some.

"We got lucky yesterday, Dude. Those thunderstorms passed right on by us to the north, and all we got was some screaming noise. Probably catch it all today, eh?"

Corcoran watched a small herd of antelope make a dash across the road, racing the wind with their graceful leaps and bounds. "Wonder what it would be like to run like that, Dude? Think you could catch 'em?" He chuckled and saw the rocky outcrop where the trail to Antelope Valley turned southeast.

He spent a full ten minutes looking over the ground

and not finding any tracks that might be considered fresh. "I think I'm here first, Mr. Doolin, and that means you lose." He found a spot high in the rocks where he could see for some distance to the west. The sun was moving well passed its zenith and would soon be in his eyes.

Dude was tethered in some scrub brush and grass, and Corcoran climbed up to his nest. "Come on, you thievin' killer, I'm waitin' for ya."

On a rise half a mile behind, Butch Clemons and Ed Reason pulled up and watched the activity. "He's gonna wait for this Doolin feller to ride into an ambush, Ed," Clemons said. "Let's get off the trail to the south and see how close we can get."

"Yeah, like rifle range close," Reason chuckled. "Wonder if we might be better off helping this Doolin guy instead of waiting for Corcoran to kill him."

"No, I don't think so," Clemons said. "We got enough trouble with them cows. Let's stick to our original plan."

Reason didn't like that idea but didn't say anything. He wondered just what kind of man this Brad Doolin was. *That old rancher said he was wanted for killing two lawmen and a rancher and his family. I could ride with a man like that. A bank robber and killer. I like that instead of being a cattle rustler. Ain't enough money in rustlin' and too damn much work.*

Shorty Evans wiped sweat and dust from his face and turned in the saddle. "These are definitely Doolin's tracks, Sheriff. I'd guess we've made up some time and are probably about an hour behind him. He's just about across the Smoky Valley by now."

"Good, Shorty." Sheriff Giles Murphy let Evans lead the posse across the Toyabe Range because of his tracking ability and was now ready to lead the charge. "Let's pick up the pace, men. Get that bastard in our sights before sunset. There's a good spring about ten miles in front of us. We'll water and rest the horses and then ride hard for the kill."

Doolin was at that springs, watching his back trail, eating a great chunk of roasted beef and drinking from rancher Harley's brandy. "I'll be in those mountains outside Eureka late tonight if I can keep up this pace." He was far from those mountains, wouldn't be there for at least another day. He had about twenty miles to go before reaching the cutoff to Antelope Valley where he planned to camp, thinking it was just outside Eureka.

The ride through open range land with a rolling sea of sage and rabbitbrush, stands of piñon pine and juniper, and outcropping rocks was tedious at best for Doolin, and it was late in the day when he saw the rocky hillside where the road branched some two or three miles off. "Hope there's water close to those rocks," he muttered.

CHAPTER NINE

Corcoran was laying in some wood for a fire when he spotted the dust a couple of miles to the west. He high-tailed it to his post in the rocks, pulled his telescope out and found what he was looking for. "There you are, Mr. Brad Doolin. You just keep right on comin' this way." Corcoran made sure both his rifle and revolver were fully loaded and ready and kept a close eye on Doolin as he rode into the ambush.

"That man's tired and so's his horse," Corcoran murmured. "Well, he's gonna get a nice long rest at the end of a rope when I'm through with him. I know lawmen would simply shoot him out of the saddle, him killin' lawmen and all, but I do believe the man should get his trial. Sure as all get out, the man's guilty, but the law is the law."

Would Corcoran simply let him get in range and drive him out of the saddle with a big slug from his rifle? As much as he might want to, the answer was no. Doolin was a known killer of the worst kind. A back shooter, a man who guns down lawmen, and one who doesn't care if the victim is a lady and mother.

"No, Mr. Doolin, I won't gun you down. I'll offer you the chance to give yourself up, give you a chance to stand trial, and then let someone else hang your bloody body high. So, Mr., just keep riding toward me." His voice was deep and soft, the way he spoke to lovely ladies, and he cradled his rifle tight to his shoulder, bringing the sights down on his target, still many hundreds of yards off.

The rocks in the jumbled pile stood at least fifty feet above the main road which circled them to the north, and Doolin spent considerable time looking behind him, hoping not to see a plume of dust. He remembered this intersection and also thought that he was still another day from Eureka.

"I can make a camp near that cathedral of rocks for tonight and make Eureka late tomorrow." He muttered just as a splash of dirt and rock were thrown up in front of his horse. And then the crack of the rifle split the air around him. He jerked his horse to a stop and was about to spin him around and race off into the waiting desert.

"Freeze or die," the voice bellowed out from thirty yards or so in front of him, and Doolin spun the horse and grabbed for his Colt. The rifle spoke again, and Doolin fell to the ground but held onto the horse's reins. Corcoran raced down out of the rocks in time to kick a pistol out of the outlaw's hand.

"My heart says to kill your ugly butt, mister, but this badge I'm wearin' says you're coming with me to face a jury of your peers. You might just consider yourself lucky," Corcoran sneered. "Oh, by the way, you're under arrest."

The heavy bullet tore Doolin's right shoulder to shreds leaving the man with his arm just hanging useless. "We'll get you patched up enough to get you to jail. Get up, Doolin, and walk that sorry horse of yours over to my camp." He picked up Doolin's pistol and shoved it in his waistband.

It took great effort for the man to get to his feet and Corcoran offered no help. "Probably hurts some, eh? Told ya not to move, dummy. Come on, walk, dammit," Corcoran snarled, pushing Doolin along. "We got about an hour of sunlight left, and I want your arm fixed enough that I don't have to bring a body back to town. Man gets tired of bringing bodies back."

Doolin hadn't said a word since being shot, just glared at the lawman poking him, shoving him, and talking mean. *Where the hell did he come from? How does he know who I am? I gotta get out of this fast.* He was already weak from loss of blood, couldn't feel his arm at all, and had no answers to his questions. *The rifle's on the saddle, but with one arm, it won't do me much good. I got that knife in my boot, and you'll die soon, lawman.*

"That sound like rifle shots?" Giles Murphy held up the posse, pointing down the long road to the great stand of rocks. "Two distinct shots, men. Let's ride," he yelled, kicking his horse into a full run.

Jake Oxford along with Shorty Evans and Aaron Snider had a hard time keeping up, and Snider, leading the pack animals, pulled up and just followed along. "Lots of dust out there, Doolin," Corcoran said. "Looks like Giles Murphy and his posse are gonna join us for supper."

Corcoran had Doolin's legs tied off, his hands tied behind his back, despite the wounded shoulder, and walked out onto the road. He held his rifle in two hands high above his head, something he learned from old Pappy Somerset. The army uses that signal to tell whoever is coming on fast that you're a friend. "Hope Murphy knows what this means," he chuckled.

Murphy and the posse rode up fast and brought their horses to a stop in a cloud of dust. "Corcoran, that you?" Murphy yelled, jumping from the saddle. "Chasing Brad Doolin, you seen him?"

"You must have known I was having roast beef for supper, Murph. Yeah, I got your man back in the rocks there. Had to shoot him, but he'll live. Bring your boys on in," Corcoran said, leading Murphy and the posse into his camp.

"Didn't kill him, eh? That's a shame."

"Reading your wire, I surely did want to, but, well, you know, he didn't go for his gun. Like the rat he is, he tried to run. So I blew half his shoulder off. He'll live."

Oxford took charge of doctoring Doolin after Snider arrived with the packs, and Shorty, Murphy, and Corcoran took care of all the animals, brought in firewood, and put together a pretty good meal. "He's my prisoner, but we're still in your jurisdiction, Murphy. I guess it's your call."

"We'll ride back to Austin in the morning, Corcoran. His crimes come from Humboldt and Lander Counties, not Eureka, but I'm mighty glad you nailed him. What's your plan?"

"I'll ride on back home. Spread the word that Doolin's out of the picture. I got a couple of rustlers to work on. You got more than enough people to keep that fool under control."

The horses were tied to a long line, Doolin, after his doctoring, was fed and then tied away from the group. With his shoulder in such bad shape, there was little chance of the man getting at the hidden knife in his boot or escaping. "Think we should post a guard during the night?" Corcoran asked. He knew he wouldn't, but it was Murphy's call.

"Naw. He ain't goin' nowhere, and besides, if he does try, we'll shoot him dead and be over with it all." There were chuckles around the fire and with a fine spread of mid-summer stars glaring at them, they turned in.

"How many of them are there, Reason?" Butch Clemons and Ed Reason had crawled as close to Corcoran's camp as they dared, watching the activity.

"Looks like five including Corcoran. You got a plan?"

"I don't know, Ed. What we talked about ain't gonna happen. What are you thinkin'?"

"When it's late and damn dark, we could sneak in and let their horses loose, free Doolin, and ride off. That's what I'd like to do." Reason had that thought the minute they found out that Doolin was in custody. *If I save Doolin, I know he'll want me to ride with him. Robbin' banks and holding up coaches is sure better than rustlin' them damn cows.*

"We'd lose all them steers, Ed. I don't know," he almost stammered.

"Suit yourself, Butch. I'm gonna save Doolin. Them cows more important to you, then ride off. I'll take care of Doolin, and maybe get to kill me a lawman or two in the process. Particular, Corcoran." His anger was always close to the surface, and Butch Clemons saw it coming. Reason had no compassion for anything, would kill before saving, seemed to want to kill and would strike out at the least provocation. In fact, Butch Clemons was afraid of the man.

"That's fine, Ed. I'll see you on the trail sometime." He crawled back to his horse and carefully led the saddled-up horse far enough back from Corcoran's camp so he wouldn't arouse anyone, and rode off in the night, nice and slow. *This ain't the time for that posse to hear me riding off or to get Ed Reason angry enough to shoot me. That was a mistake lettin' him talk his way into my little plans. I ain't lookin' to kill nobody, just pick up a few steers to sell.*

Reason crawled back to their camp, re-tied his horse, and poured some coffee and whiskey into a tin cup. He heard Clemons ride off. "Man wasn't cut out to be an outlaw." He waited until very late, slowly crept out of camp, trailing his saddled horse, and got as close to Corcoran's camp as possible. He spotted Doolin, trussed up to a large rock, several yards from where the others had their bedrolls spread out. He worked his way around the camp to where all the horses were tied off on a long line and noticed that they had not posted anyone near them.

Reason worked his way into the horses and un-tied one, slipped a bridle on, and led him quietly over to his horse. "Getting a saddle on him might not work," he mumbled and moved quietly back toward Doolin. The night was pitch black, with the only light coming from stars and the slowly dying fire.

The posse was spread around the fire, hadn't posted a guard, and Reason crawled slowly up to Doolin, nudged him gently, whispering, "Quiet, now. Quiet." Doolin came awake instantly and grabbed at Reason with his good arm. Reason put his hand over Doolin's mouth. "I'm a friend. Let's get you out of here," he whispered. He got the outlaw untied from the rock, pulled the ropes from his legs, and they crawled toward their horses.

The crawl through rough ground, over large stones and

gravel, took its toll on Doolin. He was stifling moans as they reached the horses and he had to have help getting to his feet. "Lost a lot of blood," he said. "Don't know you."

"No, but I'm glad to meet you," Reason said. "Heard about you runnin' this way and thought you might need help. We'll talk more when we're clear of that posse."

Reason helped Doolin onto the saddled horse when it whinnied loud and long. Murphy, Corcoran, and Shorty Evans were on their feet, weapons in hand as the outlaws whooped their horses into a full run. Ed Reason picked that moment to fire two shots from his revolver into the campsite, putting one slug into Aaron Snider's leg.

"Got one of 'em," he howled. "Ride for all your worth, Doolin. They'll be on us faster than lightnin'."

Murphy and Corcoran ran for their horses, had saddles wrenched down, and were on their mounts in moments. Shorty Evans yelled at Oxford to take care of Snider, and raced for his horse, now jumping, trying to chase after those running off. Luckily the long line held, and Evans got saddled and mounted quickly.

Racing a horse at a full run in the pitch dark is not the smartest thing to do, and it was Corcoran who slowed down to a fast-paced lope. "No sense killin' ourselves, Sheriff. Let them kill themselves. It'll be easier for us."

Giles Murphy had to laugh bringing his horse to the slower pace. "You got a way about you, Corcoran. Where they headin' and who was it broke Doolin away?"

"This road, of course, leads to Eureka. Who would know Doolin would be runnin' this way?" Then he remembered Butch Clemons and Ed Reason. "I was followed out of town by a couple of men I'm sure are cattle rustlers, Giles. Butch Clemons and Ed Reason. Heard of them?"

"I have now," Murphy laughed. "Wonder how Doolin got tangled up with rustlers? How far we got to go?"

"It's an all-day ride to Eureka, Murph, and the sun won't be up for another couple of hours at the least. There are some ranches spread out on the way, and if those two see lights, it might be bad for whoever's home. I'm sure they won't get off the main road, though, not when it's this dark."

"I only heard two horses ride off and you said you were being trailed by two rustlers. Wonder where number three might be?" Giles Murphy said.

It was several hours later, Shorty Evans had caught up, and they saw light coming from the Cornell ranch-house. "That's Johnny Cornell's place," Corcoran said. "He has a wife and teenage daughter. That light's a beacon, Giles. We better stop and see if they've heard anything."

"How's that shoulder holding up, Doolin?" Ed Reason and Doolin had slowed their horses to a comfortable lope after the mad dash from the camp. Doolin's shirt was hanging off his good shoulder, and the bandaged one was bleeding through. "I'm sure they're following, and it's a long way to Eureka. There's a couple of places along the road where we can hole up for a short time."

"Don't much believe in holin' up, stranger, but in this case, it might be the right thing to do. That boy back there did a good job doctorin' my wound, but it hurts like hell and will for some time to come.

"What are you thinkin', riding into a ranch or something?" Doolin was trying to size up this stranger who saved him from the posse. Why would a stranger do that? Who was he and what is he trying to gain from this? He had a lot of questions and no answers. "It ain't a smart thing to do, ride into Eureka. That sheriff chasing me probably warned all the towns. They're looking for me for sure. Find a ranch and hole up?"

"I had that in mind, but one of the men in that posse is a deputy named Terrence Corcoran, and he knows this country inside and out. No, I know a little canyon about five hours or so in front of us where there's water and shelter. Can you make another five hours or so?"

"With those bastards riding down on us? Yeah, I might grumble some, but I'll make it. I heard Murphy talking to that Corcoran. Corcoran's got a mean streak in him and convinced Murphy it would be easier to kill me than bring me in.

"What's your name and why'd you save my skinny butt?" Doolin wouldn't help anyone under any circumstances and was more than baffled by all this. "If you lookin' to rob me of what I've got, you got a lot of thinkin' to do. My left hand is still good and mighty fast, stranger." His eyes were narrowed, and he had an ugly look on his face, that left hand reached over and he realized he wasn't armed.

"You ain't got a gun, Doolin," Reason snickered. He took a little pleasure seeing the brief look of fright on Doolin's face. "Don't worry, I ain't lookin' to rob you. I want to ride with you. I heard about the bank job and the killins and I ain't been gettin' nowhere rustlin' a few steers around the valley. I want to make some real money.

"My name's Ed Reason. I've done time for small-time stuff. I'm fast, good shot, and ain't afraid of big old tough men wearin' badges," he tried to chuckle through his bragging. "I'd like to ride with someone like you, rob banks and coaches, and get some real money in my pockets."

"You done me good, Reason. Let's find someplace to hole up, and we'll talk about it." Doolin wanted to laugh right out at Reason but also knew he was in a bad place with the busted-up shoulder and possibly being caught by that posse. "Someplace where we can get to food and water, and be able to defend if that group trails us in."

You ain't gonna live long enough to join me, you proud little fool. You'd be another Sandy Whiting, an anchor around my neck.

"Hope you like beef," Reason said. He was going to ride to the canyon where he and Butch Clemons had their rustled cattle penned up. A small cabin stood back in a shelter of pine trees, there was a spring high up on the side of the mountain that ran year-round and provided water for the cattle, and they had wood stacked for the next winter's season.

"I got us a place that even Corcoran doesn't know anything about."

"Those lights over there a ranch?" Doolin was pointing to lamp-light coming from the Cornell ranch.

"John Cornell's place. They were warned about you coming into the territory by Corcoran. He's got armed buckaroos waiting for you. We'll just ride on by and head for my canyon. Those following us will surely stop to talk to Cornell giving us even more time to get well hid."

"I could use some doctorin'," Doolin almost moaned. "I guess you're right, though. Specially if they were warned that I was comin'." The moan turned to a slight chuckle, and the men rode on into the long morning hours.

"It's a little tricky riding into the canyon, and we'll make it even more so. Don't want to leave a sign that we're going in. After we get well past Cornell's ranch, we can stop for a short time, have some water, and be on our way."

"What do you mean by tricky?"

"Kinda like around and about instead of straight in. The canyon is hidden by large stands of pine and cotton-wood, and I don't ever ride straight in, rather go through a field of rocks and boulders, scrub brush, and aspen groves. Nobody's ever followed me in."

The sun wasn't quite up, but it was light enough for Butch Clemons to see the two riders pass by. He had ridden hard for an hour or so and then pulled off the main road into a stand of pine trees. His thoughts were to stay as alone as possible, as much out of sight of anyone as possible, and ride for his herd later in the day. He was just laying his head on the saddle when Doolin and Reason rode by at a gentle lope.

CHAPTER TEN

"Hello, the ranch. This is Corcoran," he yelled well before he got close enough to get shot. "There's three of us, Johnny. We're all wearing badges." He laughed in case Cornell thought he was being held or something.

"All right, Terrence. Ride in slow," Cornell yelled back. "Me and Adell got shotguns and the coffee's boilin'."

"Could use some of that." They tied off and tramped into the Cornell kitchen, smelled fresh coffee, and sat around the big family table. "Chasin' that feller I told you about," Corcoran said. "Hope this means you haven't seen or heard from him."

"Tell him about those two ruffians that came by yesterday," Marvell said.

"Two fellers stopped by just after you left, said they were looking to buy some fresh heifers, but I wasn't too sure about that. One of 'em called himself Clemons. You know 'em?"

"I believe they're responsible for Doolin being on the loose, John," Corcoran said. "I caught the fool, even shot him, but someone sneaked into camp and freed him. We're on the chase. If you folks haven't seen or heard anything, then they be well in front of us.

"Thanks for the hot coffee and we'll get back on the chase." Hands were shook, smiles exchanged, and Murphy led the three of them back out to the main road.

"You be careful, Terrence," Marvell said, quietly, smiling at the big man. *Hurry back you wonderful man and tell me you're fine. If you get wounded, let me be the one to make you well,*

"Nice family," Murphy said. "Glad they're safe. That girl sure has her eyes set on you, Corcoran," he chuckled. "Will those two we're chasing ride right into Eureka?"

"I doubt that, Giles. Ed Connors has two other deputies, and I'm sure they're primed for a fight. If that was Reason and Clemons that took Doolin, they'll head to a little canyon about ten miles or so this side of town. It's up in the mountains a ways. I've been watching a small herd of rustled cattle up there, hopin' to catch those two trying to move them.

"It's a good little fortress, and I'm sure it's well fortified with weapons and food. Will those two we left behind come this way, Murph, or did you send 'em back to Austin?"

"They'll be with us as quick as they can. They'll follow our tracks. Snider's a good tracker, and that kid from Humboldt County ain't bad, either. Don't know which one was shot. They're probably already on the road. We'll leave a good sign for 'em."

"Reason knows this country well," Corcoran said. "We're lucky they hightailed while it's still dark. They almost have to stay on this main road, at least until sun-up. We need to make some time."

They put their horses in a fast trot that eats miles.

Buckaroos making their big circles can often make sixty
miles in a day at that pace. "It'll be late in the day before
we get anywhere near that canyon." Corcoran and Murphy
spent a great deal of time doing their best to see the still
fresh tracks of the two horses in front of them. "Let's hope
we see their tracks if they should drop off this road to pull
an ambush or go cross-country."

An hour later, Shorty Evans spotted where Clemons
rode off into the trees. "Looks like someone, not our two
main people, rode up into those trees, Sheriff."

"Yeah," Murphy said. He stepped off his horse and
walked over to where the tracks came back onto the road.
Down on his haunches, he used his fingertips to push
some dirt and gravel around a bit. "He came back down,
too, and very recently. His new tracks are much fresher
than those of Doolin."

"Wonder if maybe Clemons and Reason split up somehow?" Corcoran saw that the three they were trailing were
not riding together. "We better keep our eyes open for an
ambush, Murph. Somebody's holding back, letting the two
others get well ahead of us."

"Yup," is all Murphy said.

"I don't understand," Shorty Evans said. "Why would
one man hold back like that?"

"Probably gonna try to hold us back some, slow us
down some, so the other two can get well hid. Or full out
ambush and hope to kill us," Corcoran explained. He
looked at Murphy wondering why a deputy of his wouldn't
know that. Murphy scowled and just shrugged his
shoulders.

"Let's ride," Murphy snarled.

They rode hard on a good road for another hour or
more, watching the sky lighten and then the sun come

blasting into another hot summer day. They were just cresting a rise when Corcoran spotted a single rider ahead of them, about a mile off. "He don't know we're comin'. Let's just keep this pace and not scare that buzzard into a run."

With the dips and rises in the road, the turns around rocky points and draws, it was another hour before Butch Clemons saw that he was being followed. "Damn," he muttered and wondered what he should do. Should he run? Why? He hadn't done anything wrong. Were that Corcoran and that other sheriff? "Damn," he repeated.

He knew Corcoran was already getting too close to his rustling operation, knew that if he tried to run, there was nowhere to go. He sure couldn't go to that canyon now, not with them following. He finally decided to just slow down to a walk and let those riders catch up, which they did quickly.

"Butch Clemons, pull up. This is Corcoran," he yelled, and Clemons stopped his horse and turned in the saddle. "Where's your partner?"

"Don't know, Corcoran. We split it up last night."

"You got a bunch of explainin' to do, Clemons, so we'll ride along here, and you talk. You lie to me, and I'll shoot you in the knees, first. Start with leavin' Johnny Cornell's ranch after telling me you were heading for Eureka."

Giles Murphy pulled his horse along the right side of Clemons with Corcoran riding on the man's left. Shorty Evans dropped behind, and Clemons knew he better speak the truth, or one of 'em would shoot him dead for sure.

"We heard you were looking to catch a bank robber and killer and decided to follow," he began, and Corcoran laughed right out.

"To follow, so you could help this killer, eh?"

Clemons had to take a couple of deep breaths, swallow some, and tried to explain. "My plan was to let the killer kill you, and then we would kill him and get the reward."

"Didn't think about just trying to help me catch the man?" Corcoran asked and chuckled.

"They ain't no reward," Murphy snarled. "So why not just help Corcoran?"

"Well," Clemons stammered some. "Ol Ed Reason don't much care for you, Corcoran. That's why."

"It's a good thing for you that we're in a hurry to keep on riding," Corcoran said. "If we were standing on the ground right now, I'd pound your head some. I kinda 'spect you know why we're riding kinda hard and fast." He wanted to reach out and smack Clemons but didn't. "What made you and Reason split up?"

"I ain't never done nothin' worse than pick up a few stray steers, Corcoran. I didn't want to get mixed up with a bank robber and killer. I just left before Reason did anything. Slept in the rocks back there in a stand of trees. Reason always wants to shoot somebody, wants to be a big-time outlaw. He woulda shot me 'cept the shot would have woke you boys."

Corcoran was shaking his head, looked over at Murphy and chuckled. "I don't know why, but I actually believe you, Butch. Well, so you know, Reason did set Doolin free, and the two are racing toward Eureka as we speak. He also shot a deputy, so he is a real outlaw now." Corcoran looked over at Murphy again, still shaking his head.

"Near as I can figure out, you ain't broke the law yet, Clemons. I don't think we got no hold on you, so we're gonna ride on and settle our score with Doolin and Reason. They're probably heading for that little cabin of yours, back in that hidden canyon, eh? Well, so are we. So long, Butch."

They put their horses in a fast trot, and Clemons rode on at a walk, a dumb look on his face. "Damn," he whispered. "He knows about my little herd. Damn." Dreams do disappear quickly out in the desert on a cold summer morning.

"How you feelin? We got at least another ten miles to go, Doolin." Ed Reason had to prod the man often to keep up. Doolin was bleeding through the bandages, needed water and food, and was fighting to stay in the saddle. Corcoran's rifle bullet smashed into Doolin's shoulder about at the point where the arm bone joins the shoulder bone, and the damage was frightful. Bones shattered from the impact, and muscle was ripped free. If there had been a doctor about, more than likely the arm would go.

"That bullet really tore things up, Reason, but I'll make another ten. When do we get off the main road? Those boys gotta be comin' on us hard." He wasn't about to tell Reason or anyone else just how much he was hurting. It was all he could do to hold in the screams that ached to be free.

"There's a churned-up wash comin' up in a few miles, all filled with gravel and rocks. We can ride up that wash a mile or so and drop into a stream bed that will lead us into the canyon. We'll turn into the wash as if we're going north, then turn back in the gravel and rocks and head south. Maybe those fools will follow it north. Ridin' in the gravel and rocks will make it hard for them to follow."

"Is there another way out of this canyon that you're so proud of? Gettin' boxed in like that, ain't good." He could almost see the little stone cabin he had in the mountains north of Golconda, with that trail over the ridge and out of the canyon.

"There's a game trail I've used often that leads up and out. Not a hard ride, and it gets you into open country high in the mountains south of Eureka. It sounds like you got some kind of plan."

"You heard of the Ward mining country? It's gold and silver country about sixty or so miles south of that big copper strike. Lots of gold being moved. Stage lines carrying gold and passengers with gold. That's where I'm heading. Don't want to get stuck in a canyon I can't get out of."

"That's a long ride. Ward's a couple of hundred miles from here. You can't make a ride like that with your shoulder all busted up."

"Don't you tell me what I can or can't do, Reason. That's where I'm goin'. You done me good, but don't try to tell me what to do or I'll shoot you dead."

Reason saw the anger, felt his own anger at the words, but had to smile when he remembered that Brad Doolin wasn't wearing a sidearm, didn't have a rifle, and couldn't fight if he had to. "Don't mean no disrespect, Doolin," he said. "That line of willows up ahead there is that wash and draw where we'll make a well-marked turn to the north."

"I know what you're sayin', Murph, but you gotta listen to me." Corcoran, Murphy, and Shorty Evans were standing in the middle of a rocky draw looking at hoof prints leading north. "Ed Reason is trying his best to make you believe he's riding north. This draw, if we ride south, will take us to a little spring fed creek that will lead us right into Reason's rustling hideout."

"Sure do want to follow those tracks north," Giles Murphy snapped back. "Well, this is your country, I'll go along with this, but if we come to that creek, and there ain't no prints, I'm gonna shoot you."

"Don't do that, Giles," Shorty Evans said. He walked to the south side of the main road, still in the wash, and walked south for about fifteen feet or so. "Lotta rocks tumbled about here, Giles. They're riding south for sure."

"Let's follow, then," Murphy said.

"Glad to know you ain't gonna shoot me." Corcoran laughed, mounting old Rube.

"Ground was still wet where the rocks were turned," Evans said. "Those yahoos aren't too far in front of us. We need to leave a sign for Snider and Oxford."

Corcoran broke some sagebrush off and brushed out the outlaw trail leading north and made sure all their horses gave clear evidence that they were riding south. "That should be plain enough. We don't want to ride too fast through these rocks, Murphy. We'll be making a lot of noise if we do."

"Yeah, nice and easy and watch for a possible ambush. How much light we got left, Corcoran?" They had been riding hard since well before sunrise, only stopping the two times, once at the ranch, and then when they caught up with Clemons. They only slowed down a few times to let the horses catch their breath.

"We'll make the mouth of the canyon before dark. Good place to camp and then scout our way in slow and quiet in the morning." He was pointing off to the southeast where two sets of ridges dropped down to the valley floor, marking the entrance to the canyon.

"Doolin's gunshot. Think he'll be able to fight? The rifle shot did some serious damage. I don't think he has a weapon, either," Corcoran snickered.

"He's sneaky and cruel, Corcoran. He'll figure a way to fight." Murphy was remembering his deputy being bushwhacked at the springs, and how Hanley and his wife died in the kitchen of their home. "Yeah, he'll fight."

CHAPTER ELEVEN

Freshwater from the stream, good grass for the horses, and a fire for the meat, they picked up at John Cornell's ranch made for a good camp on a hot summer evening. "Those prints stand out like flags, Corcoran," Shorty Evans said, walking along the stream bed. "They ain't much worried about being followed."

"They're outlaws, Shorty. Outlaws ain't smart. They be dumb. If they was smart, they wouldn't be outlaws." They laughed and made other crude comments, passing Jimmy Henderson's bottle of bourbon around the campfire. *Murphy's putting a lot of stake in this Evans.* Corcoran was putting together this posse he was riding with.

Murphy's a good man, but I'm not sure of Evans. His deputy Snider is a town lawman, but he is a lawman. The youngster from Humboldt County is sharp. He's the kind of man you can depend on. This might wrap up tomorrow, and it might not. Would they trap Doolin and Reason in that little cabin? Would there be a fierce firefight? *Ya gotta trust the men you're fightin' with, and I'm just not sure of the Evans feller.*

"Do we ride in or do we walk in?" Murphy brought

Corcoran back to reality. "You been into where you say they have the cattle pens and cabin. Now would be a good time to give us the layout, Corcoran."

Corcoran was down on his hands and knees and wiped away a clean area on the ground in front of the fire. "This is how the canyon is laid out," he said. He took a twig and drew out the cabin, meadow, and stream. "The mountainside broadens out quite a bit as you get higher in, and the cabin and pens are off to the west here. The cabin is surrounded by aspen and cottonwood, has a door on each end, and has two windows on each side. There are two rooms in the cabin, so each room has a window on each side. It's long and narrow.

"It was built as much for defense as for comfort many years ago by one of the first families to settle in this area. I wish I could tell you that we'll be able to shake them out fairly easy, but it ain't gonna be that way. I'm sure that Butch Clemons and Ed Reason have plenty of guns and ammo, and I know they have lots of food."

"You say this canyon broadens into a wide meadow," Murphy said. "Is there a road or trail out of that meadow? Someplace they could run? That's how Doolin got away from the Humboldt boys. They had a road out."

"No road or trail except for game trails which wander about," Corcoran said. "It's a wide and deep bowl, with a tilted but flat bottom. Excellent pasture for those rustled steers. They're not really trapped but the country going out the high side is rough."

He was interrupted by the sound of horses moving along the creek bed. All three dove for cover pulling guns as they did. "Hello, the camp," came a cry from thirty yards or so out. "It's Snider and Oxford."

"Ride on in, boys. Glad you could make the party," Corcoran called back.

Murphy helped Snider climb down from the saddle while Corcoran and Shorty helped with the horses. "Get you bad, did he?" Murphy had Snider up by the fire, looking at the man's wounded arm.

"Just a scratch, really. Oxford got the bullet out, and it's patched up fine. I can fight if that's what you're askin'. I don't like gettin' shot and most surely don't like the man that shot me." He had a wry look to his face; his jaw was set, and his eyes were full of dark anger. "I do plan to get even, Sheriff."

Murphy had to chuckle and said that's exactly what he was asking. "We'll be going in before first light. As far as we know, it's just the two of 'em, Ed Reason and Brad Doolin, and Doolin's shot up bad."

"Good," Snider laughed. "You boys left us a good trail to follow. Hope you got something to eat. We didn't stop but once, at that ranch." He looked over at Corcoran. "That young girl sure is pretty, Mr. Corcoran, and she does have a great liking for you."

That brought guffaws from everyone and a deep blush to Corcoran. "A bit too young, boys," is all he said.

"How is it this Reason fellow knew that you had captured Doolin, Corcoran?" Jake Oxford was squatted next to the fire looking at the diagram of the valley. "Seems kinda strange to me. I've been on his trail since he robbed the bank in Winnemucca, and he sure ain't stopped nowhere to send for help."

"Reason's a two-bit, wanna-be outlaw who found out I was chasing Doolin." Corcoran poured another cup of coffee and laced it with some good bourbon. "Where we're goin' in the mornin' is where Reason and his partner pasture their rustled cattle. Right now, Doolin needs Reason only because of his wound."

"Strange how things tie together sometimes, ain't it?" Oxford poured some coffee and laced it well, too. "Doolin's gang grabs an old lady for a hostage and throws her in the river racing out of town. Everyone else he's run into has been shot. Most have ended up dead. Why didn't they keep the old lady? Why ain't she dead?"

"That's the sign of good lawman, Jake Oxford," Murphy piped up.

"Why do you say that?" Shorty Evans grumbled.

"Cuz he's askin' questions that can't be answered. Means he's gonna shake as many trees as necessary to find the answers," Corcoran said. The look on Evans' face told him that the man knew not what was just said.

Small talk, a warm fire and a few generous tastes of good bourbon, and the posse fell into their bedrolls for a welcome sleep. Corcoran was up first, well before any light, and got the fire stirred up. "Time for a good fight, boys. Some side meat, hot coffee, and check your weapons." He laughed, walking around kicking everyone up. "It's a beautiful morning, you dolts. Up, I say.

Come on Shorty, get your skinny butt out. We're on a killin' mission, not a vacation. Rack it out," Corcoran growled, giving the man an extra jab with the toe of his boot. Murphy fought back, Oxford just grunted, and Snider eased his wounded self all the way to his feet.

"I don't much care for mornings, Corcoran," Murphy said. "So, if this is what I'll be looking forward to each day, I say, to hell with it. Doolin can go free." He was getting his boots on and strapping his gun belt all the time he was talking. Corcoran handed him a mug of boiling coffee. "That's better. You'll live to see another day, Corcoran."

"Give me trouble, and I'll just go home," Corcoran chuckled. "You're the one chasing him, not me."

"Actually, it's Jake Oxford what's chasing him," Murphy laughed. "Maybe we should both just go home."

"Ain't gonna happen," Oxford popped off. "You're both in it, and you know it. Neither one of you will let some young wolf-pup like me bring a mean old criminal like Brad Doolin in and get all the glory," he whooped in laughter.

"You boys just keep up the joshing. I'm the one getting Doolin. Ain't gonna let no low-down outlaw shoot me and get away with it," Aaron Snider said. He wasn't laughing.

"So, this is what you've been braggin' about all day, eh?" Doolin and Reason rode through the trees and the narrow canyon entrance into a broad meadow with a running stream cutting it in two. The cabin stood off to their right, half hidden in the trees, and a small herd of about fifty pairs were grazing in the good summer grass.

Reason guessed he had actually been braggin' some about the place but didn't like to hear it said. "Easy to defend and lots of food and water," he growled. "Let's get to the cabin, and I'll see what I can do about that shoulder."

Reason was stiff and sore from a day-long ride without the benefit of a saddle. "If your shoulder hurts as much as my backside, we're a pair." He helped Doolin down and aimed him toward the cabin while he took care of the horses. He grabbed a pail and filled it at the creek.

Doolin walked into the southernmost of the two rooms and found a good wood stove, a table with a couple of chairs, and a box full of canned fruit, mostly peaches.

Must have a cache of dried or smoked meat close by. He found sacks of flour, sugar, and coffee, and walked into the other room where he saw two crude bed frames with ropes and straw mattresses. "These boys have a nice set-up. Wish I could stay long enough to heal up, but that posse's gonna be here soon," he mumbled, heading back to the south room.

He was carefully looking over the area, noting everything he saw. *Two rifles, two shotguns, and boxes of ammunition along with the food are good, but I gotta know how to get out of here.* He found a Remington revolver and chuckled, checking it for a load. *Don't play games with me now, Mr. wanna-be outlaw.*

Doolin let Reason work on his shoulder, wincing from the pain. "Just where do you keep your meat, Reason? See the fruit and coffee, but no other food."

"Got us a cave out behind the corrals. Probably fifty or a hundred pounds of beef and venison in there, all smoked up."

"Better bring in more than ten pounds cuz this boy's got a hunger built up. Where's that trail out?"

Ed Reason finished wrapping the shoulder and walked to the western window. "Look up the side of the canyon to the left there. It winds all the way around the mountain and ends up crossing the ridge and dropping down the other side in an easterly direction. Ain't never seen any indication of anyone using that trail besides me. It's overgrown, lots of fallen trees, big rocks. Sure ain't no wagon road."

"Where does it go after that?"

"Across a valley and then high into the Grant Range. Those peaks are way over ten thousand feet. Probably still snow covered."

Anybody around there?" He didn't want to have to fight through small towns or big ranches.

"A couple of ranches in the White River Valley, but mostly open. We have a long run to Ward, but we'll get you fixed up first. Me and Clemons have horses, so we can make up a pack and be able to ride those two hundred miles easy."

Doolin nodded after looking out the window and watched Reason build a fire in the stove, put a pot of coffee on and head out to the meat cache. He walked to the stove and started working his shoulder around, back and forth, and up and down. *As long as he thinks it hurts like hell, that's fine. It damn well looks like it should hurt but doesn't for some reason.* A doctor would tell him that sometime tomorrow it will. He would also tell him that keeping it moving was about the worst thing he could do. Rubbing the broken ends of the bones against each other, stretching already ripped muscles, and breaking clots, so the blood flowed freely wasn't good medicine.

Corcoran's shot ripped through lots of meat, and it felt like it busted through a bone or two. The bullet ripped its way out the other side, creating a much larger wound. Between Oxford's and Reason's doctoring, there was no infection. Doolin found a cup and tried to lift the coffee pot with the injured arm and was able to, but awkwardly. *Had to get my right side all shot up, didn't I? Couldn't have been the left, could it?* He put the pot back on the stove and lifted it with his left hand and poured a cup.

He found he was able to lift the cup to his mouth with little trouble. He found a set of saddle bags in the other room and was busy filling one side with canned peaches, some flint, and a striker, and had a second pistol and ammunition on the other side, and left room for some meat. He checked the other revolver to make sure it was loaded, tucked it back in his holster and strapped the rig on, cross draw, just as Reason entered carrying a bundle of smoked and dried meat.

"Coffee smells good," Reason said. He put the meat on the table and turned to find Brad Doolin aiming a big revolver in his face. "Hey, what..." is as far as he got. Half his head was gone when his body flopped to the floor.

"Thanks for the help, Pard," Doolin sneered. He filled the other half of the saddle bag with meat and bags of money marked, Bank of Winnemucca. He was smiling as he walked out to the horse corral, found a fresh one, and worked hard to get saddled up. Everything was wrong, he found. He had to throw the saddle with his left hand, meaning he was on the right side of the horse, and the horse didn't much care for that.

Getting the cinch threaded and tied off took long minutes, and Doolin was frustrated, angry, and in pain when he finished. He walked the horse to the cabin door and tied him off, went in and grabbed the two rifles and saddle bags, got them tied on, and was riding out of the canyon on that back trail before it got dark.

His mistakes were piling up. Why didn't he let Reason live long enough to make up a pack horse? He found the trail, and as he climbed out of the broad meadow at the head of the canyon, he worked on putting a plan together. His only thoughts were the Ward mining district and finding a woman.

He said a couple of hundred miles to Ward, but it will be longer than that, going cross country. I gotta stay off main trails and away from people. Doolin may not have been among the brightest, but it was generally understood that most of the mountain ranges in Nevada ran north and south with a fertile valley separating them. *I got food, water, and guns. I'll make it. Oh, yeah, and all that bank money,* he snickered.

Money quickly slipped through his fingers after every job, with soiled doves getting most, saloons getting lots, him saving some back, none. It was the women that Brad Doolin craved. It was a little twelve-year-old that turned a thirteen-year-old Brad Doolin into the outlaw he was. She wanted two dollars, and he knocked a man in the head with an ax handle to get it for her. It wasn't her first time. It wasn't his last.

Doolin was over the top of the ridge and into wild country well before the sun settled. His camp was under some fir trees and gave him a good look to the east. "Those are big damn mountains I gotta cross." He was having second thoughts about the mining camp of Ward. Eureka was looking better and better, and then he accidentally banged his shoulder and knew he could not ride into Eureka. "They'd spot me in a second. Damn it, damn it, damn it." He almost snarled the words out.

Even though it was the 1870s, Nevada was sparsely settled, there were few roads, and those that existed ran between the few towns and villages that had grown up along the emigrant trails or led from one ranch to another. What trails there were either game trails or those used by the various Indian tribes, and seldom led to any particular destination. It was a wild and desolate country he would be riding through, and he was not prepared.

Murphy let Corcoran lead the men into the canyon. They had decided the best bet was to ride in, get a good look at the layout and spread wide for their approach to the cabin. "There's two of them, one wounded, and five of us,"

Murphy said. "Ain't no way they can defend if we come at them from five different directions."

"One thing, though," Corcoran said. "Let's not be shootin' each other."

"Damn, and I so want to," Murphy chuckled, nudging his horse forward.

The creek ran right down the middle of the canyon and took up most of the space in the narrow entrance, allowing the men to ride in the creek and make that much less noise. As the canyon walls spread and the area became a broad plain or meadow, Murphy kept them close to the west flank. "No smoke, Corcoran. Think they gathered supplies and split last night?"

"Possible," Corcoran said. "There's only game trails to follow, and that's not likely at night. Let's spread wide like we planned and move in quickly. We'll have our answer soon. Keep down and don't get shot."

They were well out of rifle range as they spread out and around the cabin. Jake Oxford went up high on the mountain in order to drop down on the cabin from the west. He was moving through big trees and came on a game trail that showed fresh horse prints. *Bet at least one of those boys is dead, and the other ran off last night.* He continued down until he could see Murphy moving in from the north.

"There's fresh horse prints leavin' out on a trail up here, Sheriff." He hollered it out and heard Murphy cuss some before moving closer to the cabin. "Bet there's a dead one inside."

"Don't get your head shot off but take a quick look if you can."

Jake Oxford crawled through the brush, broken limbs, and rocks to come up under one of the windows. He took a deep breath and eased up so he could get a look in. "Got a dead one in there, Sheriff." The cussing was stronger and louder this time, and Oxford had to chuckle. He walked around to the door and kicked it open as the rest of the posse moved in.

"What's left is Ed Reason," Corcoran said. "Looks like Doolin took a goodly supply of guns and food, too." Doolin wasn't careful in his packing, and flour, coffee, sugar, and other stuff was spilled about. "We got us a hard ride, Sheriff."

Giles Murphy sat down at the table, thinking, drumming his fingers, looking around the room. He knew as well as anyone in that room just how hard a ride they would have to make. "Any idea where Doolin might head? He's got guns and ammo, probably enough food for three days or more, and he's alone, meaning he can travel as fast as he wants."

"With that shoulder, he won't be doing any fast riding, Sheriff," Jake Oxford said. "He'll only bust it open so many times before he will have to slow down."

"He won't be going south or west, for sure," Corcoran said. "He would have to circle around Eureka to go north, and that would put him in a country that is already looking for him." Corcoran sat down across from Murphy. "You said his specialty was stagecoaches and banks, so my guess would be Eureka or one of the mining areas to our east."

Murphy laughed. "He ain't goin to Eureka, Corcoran, you know that. If he has a plan, it would be the eastern mining camps."

"That's a two-hundred-mile run, Murphy."

"Found a meat cache back in the hillside," Shorty Evans said. "Looks to be more than a hundred pounds of beef hanging back there."

"Doolin's got a good head-start on us," Corcoran said.

"We've got meat and cans of fruit. Let's tear this place apart and put together packs. We're missing coffee, beans, and flour. Find those, and we can be on the trail in an hour. Shorty, work with me, and we'll build packs for two horses. Oxford and Snider, find us the food to stuff in 'em. We'll run that bastard to ground."

"Six feet deep in the ground," Murphy growled. "I'll get the horses down here and help whoever needs help. That boy'll kill anyone that gets in his way. What about ranches if we find he is heading east."

Snider fought the pain in his leg, and he and Jake had food packs organized in quick time. "You gonna make this ride, Snider?" Jake Oxford worried about gunshot wounds and the infections that seemed to always follow.

"If it means getting a chance to shoot that bastard, I can ride for weeks, Jake. I don't care much for gettin' shot."

Nevada's population grew from Virginia City in the far west, east to Utah, following the major silver discovery, so the eastern valleys of the state were even more sparsely populated. Prospectors moved through the mountains, and brave men and women tried to tame the great intermountain desert to raise cattle and sheep.

"There are ranches in all the valleys, Giles, but spread out. Most know they're alone and don't take easy to strangers, particularly wounded ones comin' to visit. They've fought off Indians, land speculators, water thieves, you name it. They'll be wary of a single stranger riding up on their place."

CHAPTER TWELVE

It was mid-day by the time the posse rode up and over the ridge at the top of the bowl. They gave Reason a decent burial, got the packs put together, and rode out with two pack animals full. Doolin's trail wasn't particularly easy to follow, the day was boiling hot, and everyone knew they were far behind their quarry.

"I gotta get word to Ed Connors, Murph. And I'm sure not leaving out to do it."

"Shorty, ride hard to Eureka and tell the sheriff what has happened, where we are, and where we think we're going. Then get back on our trail as fast as you can. We need every gun we can get." Corcoran gave him a note to give to the sheriff.

"When we get off this little range, Murphy," Corcoran said, "we have a wide valley to cross and then climb the big Grant Range. That will be the worst country to go through. If we're lucky, we'll run Doolin down before then."

What kind of a man are we following? Corcoran had brought vicious killers to the hangman many times over the years, but this Brad Doolin seemed somewhat different. He watched an angry Shorty Evans ride off with the message.

I saw where Reason took the time and effort to help Doolin with his wounds, and that bastard said thank you with a 45-70 through the head. And that ranch family back in Austin. He's a killer with no feelings for life. Most dangerous type of fiend. Corcoran just shook his head, not coming up with any other kind of answer.

The country they rode through was steep, covered in brush and trees, with rock outcroppings constantly getting in the way. There were downed trees and slippery ground, boulders bigger than cabins to be ridden around; it was a slow ride. Corcoran's mind was working on what kind of man they were hunting.

Ed Reason broke Doolin free, apparently tended his wounds, offered him a safe place to hide, and the man shot him dead. No thoughts for anything but himself. Self-preservation. Well, Mr. Doolin, I'm gonna get you and you ain't gonna like it.

"What's in front of us, Corcoran? This isn't any kind of a well-used trail. Where are we going?" Giles Murphy could read the country as well as Corcoran and wondered if Doolin might have a plan. "That shoulder has got to be giving him hell."

"I hope so," Corcoran chuckled. "When we drop off this ridge and start working our way down out of this range, we'll come to a long wide valley. Damn near flat, Murphy, and there ain't much there. We're two days or more from that valley.

"We're high up on this range, and it'll be a long hard ride down to that valley. As set up as he is, he'll do what he can to make good time, I imagine. He'll be making for the Grant Range, and when he drops into the White River

Valley is when he might run into people. A smart man would ride right on across the valley."

"Unless he hurts enough to ask for help."

"Or demand it," Corcoran said.

"Yeah," Murphy murmured, thinking about the family back in Austin. "He simply broke through their door and shot those people in Austin, Corcoran. He didn't demand anything, simply killed and took."

It was a day off the ridge and another day across the valley to the Grant Range. They followed Doolin's trail with no trouble, but there was no actual trail he was following. He followed terrain across the valley, and game trails when he hit the mountains. "This fool hasn't sent a great deal of time in the wilderness, Murphy," Corcoran said.

"He's still tending toward the south, not holding due east as I would think if he's really heading for the Ward district. It'll take us two days to cross these mountains and drop into the White River Valley and the possibility of running onto one of the ranches.

"These people out here are damn protective of what they have. They've fought off Shoshones and Utes, rustlers and wolves for years. They won't welcome a wounded man riding alone."

"What's alone got to do with it?" Oxford asked. Jake Oxford grew up in the town of Winnemucca, never lived on a ranch, and the idea of a single man, wounded or not, coming up wouldn't have raised his awareness level a bit.

"If he rode onto a ranch, wounded and trailing a pack horse, most would rush to help him, but alone? Out here, a hundred miles or more from anywhere? He would be considered a danger, running from something. And a man like Doolin would know that."

"Well, we won't be anywhere near that valley for some time. We're getting into mighty rough and high country right now." Murphy and the rest were strung out single file working their way through large rock fields about nine thousand feet above sea level. "We still got to work our way down through the forests," he muttered. Like Eureka County, Murphy's Lander County is mountainous, with few actual roads.

The mountains of central Nevada, whether the Toyabe Range, Monitor Range, or Ruby Range, were pure wilderness with little indication that humans had been there. What trails existed were made by the wild animals of the area, not by men on horses.

"We'll still be many miles from the valley floor. If we camp late and start early, and hope Doolin's shoulder is killing him, we'll catch up in a day or two."

"Glad Shorty gets back. We're gonna need his gun, I think," Jake Oxford said.

The trail they were following moved with the terrain, probably originally a deer or elk trail and Doolin seemed to just be following along. "This man has no idea where he's going," Corcoran murmured often. They worked their way through dense forest, across spring-fed streams, around massive rock outcrops, and always angling downward.

"This wind's got a cut to it, Corcoran. If those clouds keep building, we'll be in for thunderstorms later."

"We will, Murphy, and at this altitude, it won't be rain falling on us, either. We'll keep an eye out. It's always good to remember that the guy we're lookin' for is facing the same crap. Makes me smile some, hopin' it pains him. We have the canvas to hide under if it comes to that."

Doolin rode slowly into the night stopping only when he simply couldn't see where he was going. He set up a quick camp, had some coffee and smoked meat, and wondered just what he would find on this trek a third of the way across Nevada. The idea of the Ward mining district's potential money was still the driving force. Banks and gold-laden stagecoaches would keep him moving east for as long as it took.

In eastern Nevada, the big money would have been in Elko, but Doolin knew that every sheriff east of Winnemucca was on the lookout for him. Ward was a little-known mining district well south and east of Elko, and Doolin knew there was money to be had.

"They got saloons, and that means women, and I rob banks and stagecoaches so I can have any woman I see. They love my money, and I got enough to keep them and me happy."

Not that many years ago, he thought, sitting by his little fire sipping hot coffee, this would be a cold camp. Shoshone and Ute Indians ruled this country and didn't cotton to all these people moving through and in. *Ain't Indians I'm worryin' over right now.* He took the dressing from his shoulder and tried to wash out the wounds with hot water, crying out from the pain.

Ain't got a friend left in the world, got thousands of dollars in gold and cash, and don't have any idea where I am. All because Simpson grabbed that woman and threw her in the river. Those banks in Ward better be full. The ride over the country that was seldom seen, following game trails instead of open roads, and not actually knowing where he was, was taking its toll.

He had heard the word gangrene often when men were talking about their wounds and infections and remembered that somebody said it smelled bad. He picked up the rags, crusted with blood and smelled of them, throwing them in the fire and retching.

"Oh, damn, that smells bad. I ain't gonna die out here, alone. I got money enough to demand someone fix me up." He was working himself into a rage, knowing that a bad infection always led to death. Anger was always right at the surface, his gang members had let him down, and the plans he had for spending that bank money were gone away. *I was gonna spend two days with the doves, and there better be plenty of them in Ward.*

His shoulder ached all night, pain shooting through him with every turn in the blankets, and he was up and had a fire going at first light. He boiled some water and tried to clean the wounds again but only tore scabbing away making it bleed. It was the ache, not a shooting pain, that hurt the most. He remembered from a broken arm years ago. The ache of a broken bone, different from the pain of a knife cut or bullet wound.

He cursed the pain, tore more strips off his one remaining shirt, washed out the wounds, and dressed them as best he could. One more cup of coffee and soaked meat, and he set out for another day of not knowing where he was going. He took his anger out on his horse, forcing it through thick timber, rocks, and downfall.

I gotta keep going east, was his constant mantra. He knew only that the Ward district was east of where he was. The mountains west of Ward are high and little traveled. The country between where he was and where those mountains

were was rough, the valleys mostly unsettled, the mountains mostly wilderness. He was still faced with at least
two massive ranges and large open valleys in between.

He worked his way down through forests of large pine
and fir trees, great stands of aspen, and rocky outcrops and
ledges into the broad White River Valley by early the next
evening. Doolin was in constant pain, his shoulder was
infected, and the ache in that shoulder was far stronger
than in the morning. He needed help. He found a stream
coming out of the mountains and made up camp. He again
boiled water and tried to clean out the wound, almost
passing out from the pain.

It was a long sleepless night, and he again tried to clean
out the wound in the morning. Hot water on a filthy piece
of already bloody cloth brought cries of pain across the
open plain. *I gotta get help.* Breaking camp brought moans,
cries, almost weeping from the outlaw and it was late in
the morning before he got in the saddle. The day was
already hot, thunder clouds could be seen building over
the mountains, and there was no breeze.

He followed the trickling stream well into the valley,
and it disappeared into the ground, as most coming out of
Nevada's mountain ranges do. The seep was surrounded by
cottonwood trees and willow. He rode over a rise and saw
smoke several miles in the distance. "I sure as hell don't
want to ride up there, but I gotta get some help." He
muttered and grumbled, could continually smell the infection that had set in, knew it would only get worse if he
didn't get help soon. *I gotta have something to tell 'em, though.
Ridin' in alone, all tore up like, ain't gonna set well.*

The cabin, rock-walled on the two ends and built with
rough cut timbers on the sides, was small, probably four
rooms at best, had a sod roof, and Doolin could see a

couple of outbuildings and corrals, one of which held a couple of horses. He rode slowly into the open yard and stopped about twenty-five feet or so from the cabin. *Only a few horses, I don't see a bunkhouse. One person, two at the most.* He read the ranch and hoped that whoever was there would know how to fix his shoulder.

"Hello, the house," he yelled. He saw the working end of a shotgun in the open doorway and sat very still, both his hands in plain sight. It was a sight he had seen many times before and he remembered that he had talked himself out of danger many times. He needed to this time.

"What's your business?" It was a deep man's voice, and Doolin sat still.

"I'm hurt. Need some help."

"I see the blood from here, stranger. Looks like a gunshot from here." The man was off to the side, in the shadows, and Doolin couldn't tell if he was alone. The shotgun was pointed right at him, and he sat still.

"Shot myself cleanin' my gun. I need help."

"You gotta help him, Silas. You can't just chase him off." Beverly Anderson was standing behind her husband, watching the man on the horse sway some with pain. "He's in no condition to do us harm."

"Step down and relieve yourself of that gun belt," Silas hollered. He watched Doolin fight his way to the ground and undo the belt. Doolin stumbled slowly toward the house, pain and weariness more than obvious. "Hold up right there, now. Not another step," Anderson barked.

Beverly Anderson started for the man, and Silas stopped her. "No," he said. "You, stranger, come on up on the porch nice and slow and set yourself down in that chair." The shotgun never moved from the big man's shoulder. "You ain't been working none of the ranches around here, you ain't set up for a pack trip nowhere, and you're wounded bad.

"All of that put together means you are probably running from something. The law, maybe?"

"I was trying to make Eureka before the accident. Got a job there, working for the sheriff. Need help, bad," he lied. "Been two days since the accident." The lies piled up, the wound was already more than five days old, and he sure as hell wasn't ever gonna be a sheriff's deputy. He was weak, stumbled as he tried to make the walk to the porch.

Anderson listened and became even more sure the man was an outlaw. Eureka was almost a hundred miles to the northwest, so where was this man coming from? "We'll put a fresh bandage on you, stranger, then you'll have to ride off. Beverly, put some water on to boil and rip some bandage cloth.

"You just sit in that chair and don't move. My smoke stick is loaded with buckshot." Silas Anderson was twenty-eight years old and he and Beverly, now twenty-five, home-steaded the place almost ten years ago. The years have been good some of the time and not so good other's. They had one man working for them, old Clint McAvoy, but weren't able to have children. McAvoy lived in the barn, but not today. The old range rider was out in the wide valley working the herd. The Andersons were alone.

The two grew up in the Green River area on neigh-boring ranches and ran away when her parents didn't approve of Anderson. As children of those coming into the wild frontier while it was still wild, they had a knowl-edge of how to live safe. She was still a very attractive young lady despite the hardship of homesteading in raw country.

Her straw-colored hair hung in a long-braided length

down her back, and her shoulders were wide and strong; her breasts straining some at a cotton blouse. She was wearing a long skirt that showed an enticing swell at her hips, and Doolin knew she had long legs. She was almost as tall as her husband.

Doolin watched Beverly walk into the house and remembered how long it had been since he had been with a woman. Wasn't that one of the main reasons for robbing a bank? Get pockets full of gold, and a man can have any woman he wants. He knew he wanted Beverly and he knew he had pockets full of gold. Those hips swayed with an invitation, her breasts swelled with every breath, and his lust built rapidly.

He held his busted up wing and slowly edged up the porch steps, keeping a close eye on that worrisome shotgun cradled in strong arms. "You got a nice place here," he said, trying to ease the man's thoughts. "Must take quite a crew to keep it going." It took a minute to get in the heavy chair under the cabin's front window. He was on a broad porch that spread across the face of the cabin.

"Got three men working the herd and another three in the corrals and pens," Anderson lied. *Didn't take this yahoo long to ask that question, now. Don't much care for the way his eyes were following Bev, either.* "Where you coming in from? We're a long way out, down here in the valley."

"Well, the truth is," Doolin tried to laugh a bit, "I think I got myself lost. I left Ward three days ago and thought I'd be in Eureka before now."

"Yeah, you're lost all right. You're fifty miles south of the road to Eureka. What are you runnin' from?" Anderson was tired of the lies and tales. "You ain't set up for no two-hundred-mile journey across this country, mister." He didn't say any more as Beverly came out onto the porch with a basin of hot water, some medicines, and bandage material. "Nobody rides across the Nevada desert for two hundred miles without a pack horse. What're you thinkin', I'm just a dumb old farmer out here'll believe any story you make up?"

Beverly started to walk up to Doolin, and Anderson held her back.

"Not yet, Bev." He held the big scattergun in one hand and moved a table across the porch to Doolin's chair. "Put the stuff down," he said to Beverly. "You, stranger, strip off those bandages and be quick. I want you off this place just as soon as possible."

He watched Doolin slowly take the bandages off the infected wound, crying out as each scab was broken free. "Now, move that chair around so your back is to the table, and Beverly, you work on that shoulder from behind the man. I'll shoot you, stranger, at the slightest wrong move or comment."

Doolin was sure the man meant exactly what he said, but the pain was intense, the dreaded thoughts of being back in the saddle again and was fully aroused by the sight of Beverly Andersons's swaying hips and delightful young body. He thought of offering gold and let that go but knew he wanted her bad.

He was almost out of the food he had taken from the ranch in Austin, and Beverly Anderson had something on her stove inside that smelled of heaven. Doolin was straining to come with something to say that would bring an invitation to supper. Nothing came to mind, mostly because of the pain from his wounds.

She was using a strong soap along with the hot water to cleanse the wound, and he couldn't stop crying out and moaning from the pain. Anderson seemed to snicker some at each outcry which angered the outlaw. He was almost sobbing at the pain and vowed he would kill the man as slowly as possible and have his woman before he died.

Beverly wiped the wounds dry, then spread some kind of ointment over the gaping holes before wrapping the shoulder tight. He could almost feel the pain go away as the ointment worked its way in. She stepped back and turned with a smile, nodding to her husband.

"You're patched up, stranger. Mount up and get off my place. Move it," he said, bringing the shotgun up to his shoulder. Doolin knew he couldn't run and eased himself out of the chair, stumbled down the stairs, and walked to his horse.

He reached down for his gun belt, and Anderson bellowed, "No! Leave it be right where it is."

"I can't go off unarmed," Doolin whined.

"You still got the rifle you shot yourself with," he snick-ered. "Mount up and git," he snarled. The holes in the wrong end of that shotgun looked like deep tunnels of death to Doolin as he struggled with his horse.

It took some doin, but the outlaw got in the saddle and rode off into the desert. He didn't look back, and Silas Anderson didn't move off the porch until Doolin was completely out of sight.

"Do you think he'll be back?" Beverly was picking up the bloody rags after dumping the basin of water. "He had scary eyes, Silas."

"He did, and they kept undressing you. I should have killed him. I will," he snarled, "if he does come back." He walked into the little cabin and set the shotgun next to the doorway. "That's loaded, Bev, and you know how to use it. I'm putting the rifle near the back door, and you know how to use that. Don't wait," he said. "If you see him, shoot him. I'm gonna leave a note for old Clint out in the barn."

Doolin rode back to the stream and pulled up to where he had camped the night before. He needed to make a plan, couldn't get the sight of that woman out of his mind and was almost pain-free as he lit a fire to make coffee. "After I take that woman I'll take more of that ointment," he almost chuckled.

Because of the doctoring, Doolin got his first full night's sleep since being wounded and came out of his bedroll just as the sun spread its warmth across the wide valley. He worked his shoulders about, found it still painful but not as bad as the day before, and got a good fire going. "I want that woman," he muttered, "and I want that big man dead. Can't ride in while it's light but, tonight, I'll have her."

The man was on a desperate run for freedom and showed just how stupid he was, thinking of this attractive woman instead of getting away from what he knew was a sure posse following. Was it simply a lack of intelligence? Surely an intelligent man would know he was being chased, so it was probably simple stupidity. An ignorant man can learn, a stupid man won't, and Doolin had better things to think about, such as, Beverly and killing Anderson.

He needed to know the lay of the land and rode out of camp within the hour. He rode wide of the house and made a full circle of the property before coming back to his camp. There were numerous deep ditches and arroyos, great stands of pine on the foothills, and indications of bunches of cattle being driven by one rider.

The hot summer day was coming to an end and thunderheads could be seen building over the mountains to the west as he rode into his camp. He'd been lucky in this run for freedom so far. Thunderstorms had been seen but hadn't hit where he was. This time would be different, he knew, watching the massive clouds roll over the broad plain of the valley.

Flashes of lightning and rumbling thunder filled the air, and a cooling breeze drifted across the valley. Soon rain will fall, and the desert will be filled with the sweet aroma of damp sage and desert dust.

"Sweet Beverly, you will be mine tonight," he said, getting a fire started. I'll eat, sleep for a bit, and sneak in to kill that big man before I make you mine."

CHAPTER THIRTEEN

"That is one wide valley, Corcoran," Murphy said as they rode across a ridge, still high in the mountains. "The trail Doolin left has been easy to follow, but the ride has been hell. My knees are killing me. I don't think the man has any idea where he's going. It's generally been east, but he's been shading south all day."

"He's following game trails instead of paying attention to direction. There are two ranches down in that valley, the Pine's north of where we're looking, and the Anderson's to our south. Gene Pine has a big outfit and moves hundreds of head of cattle yearly, but Anderson and his wife just barely get by."

"Think he'd stop at one of them?"

"Only if he's hurt real bad," Corcoran said. "We'll work our way into the valley by tonight and if his trail continues as it has, it will lead us near the Anderson place. I've only met Silas once, and if Doolin goes up against him, he'll lose his other shoulder."

Corcoran had to chuckle remembering the ruckus at the rail yards when a cattle buyer tried to back out of a buy. "An old stingy cattle buyer tried a fast move on Anderson once," he said to the group. "Tore that auction barn to shreds, he did. Man's got a temper and is built like a freight train. Took three of us to calm him down," he laughed.

Murphy was laughing right out as he led them off a ridge and down a long draw toward the valley. The trees were thick, and the only way down was by way of a game trail. Doolin's tracks stood out from those of deer and elk, the trail was narrow and rocky, and they were forced to ride slow and easy. "Sure be glad to get on some level ground again," Murphy chuckled.

"At least we're going straight down the side of the mountain, Murphy. I rode for an outfit that only knew one way to ride in the hills, and that was side-hillin'. Wear you out by dinner."

"Well, if you start side-hillin' on me, I think I'll shoot you, Corcoran. Might anyway, gettin' me in a mess like this."

"You came to me crying for help, Murphy," Corcoran laughed, and it took a minute before Murphy started chuckling too.

"Yup, guess I did. Shoulda just a sent a wire sayin' old Doolin was comi' your way."

"I think you did. Problem is, you followed along. It is interesting, though. Jake Oxford has a bank robbery and murder hold on him. You have three murder holds on him, and I have one. Who's gonna get him first."

"The gravedigger," Murphy snarled, then grinned.

Summer in the high mountains was generally a pleasant time with warm, not hot, daytime temperatures, cool evenings, and brisk nights. As they moved down off the high ridges, the heat increased and as they neared the valley floor, it became intense.

The afternoon wore on, and steep mountains became rolling foothills, the thunderheads were building fast, and a cooling breeze popped up. "Got some real gully-washers coming our way, I do believe," Corcoran said. "Let's find a stand of pines and build some lean-tos. Bedrolls, food, everything needs to get under something. We've gotten a little sloppy putting these packs together."

"I don't take kindly to that comment," Shorty Evans snorted. He and Snider had been given the chore of packing the two horses each day. "Snider's hurt doesn't help much, and I do my best."

"Your best has gotten sloppy, Shorty. Just like Corcoran said." Murphy snorted some leading the group into a stand of pine trees.

"I got caught in one of these down near Belmont one summer," Murphy said. "Washed away the entire camp. Took us three days to find everything. Even lost a horse to the high water."

"A little dry wash can become the mighty Missouri in minutes," Corcoran said.

Lightning seemed to come from several directions at the same time, rolling crashes of thunder fought with each other for dominance, and the rain fell in torrents for several hours. The ground shook, and little rivulets turned into roiling madness within minutes. When it ended, the sun shone as bright as mid-day despite the lateness of the day. "Look under the rocks and near the base of the trees for any dry wood," Murphy said to Oxford. Glad we got those packs in the lean-to."

"Rain that heavy is gonna just about wash out Doolin's tracks." Corcoran brushed sweat out of his eyes as he helped dismantle a lean-to. "Let's warm up and dry out best we can and get down on the valley floor before dark. We'll have to scout some in the morning to pick up his trail."

"This air is thick," Murphy said, wiping sweat from his face. "Doesn't take long for the sun to take that rain back, eh?"

"Just read your message, Silas. Thought you should know I saw tracks out some north of here and followed them. They seemed to circle the cabin, out about a mile or maybe two from it. Just a single horse."

Clint McAvoy was a string bean of a buckaroo, hard as an iron nail until a cow or a pretty girl needed help. "Somebody lookin' to know all about this place, without you knowin' about him. I got a good little herd of steers for the market drive."

"Thanks, Clint. Sit down and have some coffee and I'll tell you all about it. Looks like those thunderheads are coming straight for us today. That'll make the grass grow." Silas Anderson stoked the fire and brought the coffee pot to the kitchen table.

"Had a visitor today and he's a bad one. Anyone come riding in, kill him on sight, Mr. McAvoy. Don't give him any kind of break. Man had death written all through his eyes, and a lust for Beverly."

"I don't cotton to killin' a man, Silas. You know that. But anyone look to hurt that wonderful wife of yours is askin' to be kilt for damn sure." Clint McAvoy was nearing sixty years, had served the union and in the Indian wars, rode long Texas trails, and was fully at home on the Anderson place. He planned to die in the saddle, as he told

Silas Anderson often, a long way from four walls and a roof.

"No, sir, any man look to lay a hand on Beverly is a dead man. Those tracks I run on came from one horse, Silas. This man was alone? Probably runnin' from something."

"No pack horse, not even a saddle pack tied on. He had a bad wound right where his arm joins his shoulder, meat and bone all tore up by a bullet. Bev said it was infected, but she doctored him up good. I should have just shot the man but didn't. Hope I don't regret that."

"Don't like the sound of that, Silas. Ain't no reason for a man to ride through this long and lonely valley, alone and with no supplies, unless he's runnin' from somethin', and that makes him dangerous." McAvoy sipped his coffee and looked over to Beverly, sitting near the stove mending something. "Didn't happen to put some poison in the doctorin' stuff, did ya?"

She laughed, shaking her head. "No, Clint, but he's gonna wish I had if he don't see a real doctor soon."

"He won't. Those kind never do."

They spent the next hour just talking about how the young steers were looking, how many heifers they might be able to hold back, how many older ones would be going to market and the condition of the range. It was getting late in the afternoon when the rains came with a vengeance. Thunder shook the walls as lightning blasted the plain, and rain came like a bursting dam.

"Whooie," Anderson exclaimed. "It's about time." Beverly joined the men with a big smile, standing by the open door watching the rain pelt the dry earth. "I was worried about the garden, Silas, but not now. We'll be eating fresh corn and green beans the rest of the summer. Have to start puttin' stuff up, too."

Heavy thunderstorms are usually coupled with cold wind, and the cabin had cooled considerably in just a short time. Beverly added some wood to the fire, and both men stood next to the big stove.

"Nice day to be by the stove, eh Clint?" Anderson put even more wood on the fire, pulled a jug down from the cabinet and poured each of them a healthy dose. "Why don't you stay in here and have supper with us tonight? Don't you get tired of always being by yourself out there in the barn, cooking over an open fire?"

"It's the only life I've known, Silas. Barn's almost big enough for me to be comfortable. House is too small. Walls are too close. Too stuffed up," McAvoy said. "I gotta lay in my old bedroll, and when I open my eyes, I want to see stars, not a roof. Went two years without ever being in a building once. That was down in Texas working for an old guy who got his cattle from others if you know what I mean." He chuckled, took a long drink of coffee and a sip of whiskey. "We'd ride across the border for strays, he called 'em, and spend the next two days brandin' those strays."

"That how our herd growed a bit the last couple of years?" Silas Anderson was well aware that Clint had incorporated a few strays into their herd. He chuckled a bit and sipped some whiskey. "Old man Pine can afford missing a few now and then, but let's not make it a habit, if it's all right with you."

"Don't know what you're talkin' about, Silas," the old man said, coughing just at the right time. "No, I think I'll mosey on back to the barn, get my fires going, and watch the sunset, Silas. I'll keep a close watch," he said. He drank the last of the whiskey and washed it down with coffee, nodded to Anderson, gave Beverly a big smile, and headed out the door as the rain began to let up. *I'm gonna have to take a little ride after supper. Single rider, gunshot wound from the front? Lookin' hard at Beverly? Haven't killed a man in a long time, but it sure looks like I will tonight.*

"You're thinking that man will come back, aren't you, Silas?" Beverly was putting together supper of fried steaks and steamed corn. "I was worried that he would do something while he was here."

"It's not easy to say, but I should have killed him on sight. He is a very dangerous man, Beverly, and yes, I'm afraid that he will return. There won't be no talking this time." She could hear the pent-up anger.

A massive clap of thunder brought Brad Doolin scrambling out of his bedroll just in time to welcome heavy rain and wind. Doolin had taken the time to grab some sleep knowing he would be up most of the night. He had seen the thunderheads building but wasn't trail wise enough to do anything about it. There was no lean-to. No shelter for his gear, him, or his bedroll. He didn't move his camp to high ground, neither.

"Damn it," he yelled, gathering his belongings and not having anywhere to put them. The rain came in sheets, driven by gale force winds. The sky seemed to empty itself on his campsite, and he had nowhere to hide. He found out within moments that he had camped too close to the little creek.

It boiled over the banks, flattening the willows growing on the banks, and washing Doolin's camp downstream. He should have known that's why all those gullies and arroyos were there in the first place. Summer thunderstorms brought flash floods to the valleys every year. That's why the valleys were often lush with grasses and brush. His horse was throwing a fit, tied as he was to one of the cedar bushes and fighting high and fast water, and Doolin rushed to it, got it untied and up a rise to higher ground on the valley floor.

Just a few minutes ago, this was a peaceful little stream meandering through the valley. Now, it was an ugly, muddy, and very dangerous cataclysm. He was wet to the waist, his boots filled, and he stood in the swirling rain screaming his frustration at the winds.

All he could do was hunker down under a nearby stand of cottonwood and wait out the storm. He was rabid with anger, not at his own stupidity, mind you, but at Silas Anderson for not inviting him to stay at the ranch, at the storm for washing his camp away, for everything in the world that was conspiring to do him in. Most of all, he hated that weasel who threw the woman in the river.

He had wrenched his wounded arm bad fighting to get he and his horse out of the raging flood, and the ache got worse the more he stood in the rain. The thunderstorm ended as fast as it had started, but the heavy rains hung on for another hour or two. The creek didn't go down, and Doolin spent the rest of day walking along the flooded creek bank, retrieving his goods.

Money. My God, the bank money's in those saddle bags. He raced up and down the creek bank, tearing through knee-deep water, tripping over willow branches and slippery rocks, grabbing what he could.

The saddle wasn't destroyed, but he never found the headstall and bridle. He found his shredded bedroll, coffee pot, and finally, the saddle bags. Doolin almost did a dance when he discovered that his money from the bank job was still there. He brought everything to the stand of cottonwood trees, got enough dry wood put together to get a fire started, sat down on a rock, and cussed for ten minutes at the top of his lungs.

It was getting dark when he got himself put together enough to understand just how much trouble he was in. He found enough busted up limbs and dry wood to build a rack to hang his stuff on to dry and still keep the fire going strong. Sorted out, it was obvious he had lost a lot. Most of his meat was gone. Washed right out of that one set of bags. Most of his clothing was gone, and he would be riding a horse with a halter and ropes for bridle and reins.

"I ain't got much choice now, do I?" He snickered, kicked some rocks, and threw a chunk of wood at the fire. "I gotta raid that ranch, kill that man, and take his woman, and I gotta do it tonight. Can't wait." The pain had returned and getting his already skittish horse saddled was almost more than he could stand. It was getting very dark, and Doolin was almost drooling thinking of Beverly Anderson.

McAvoy cooked an elk steak on a grill over an open flame, settled down with his back to a rock just outside the north end of the barn. He sat just inside a three-sided shed on the north end of the barn, looking at the sunset to the west. The air was sweet with fresh rain on the valley floor, and the sunset was spectacular. Like so many who live the life of the wild and free, McAvoy was close to nature, had the soul of a poet, and a distinct dislike for evil men.

What Anderson said is pretty close to what I saw on my circle. I should have followed that trail and done the man in. He'll hit tonight, I know that and so does Anderson. Think I'll eat some and ride out a bit, see what I can see.

The stars were bright in the rain-freshened air; the warmth of the ground made the night comfortable as Clint McAvoy rode his horse quietly through the valley. He planned to circle out north and around west, before turning back to the ranch. He'd been working the cattle on this range for enough years that he didn't need much light to know where he was and what might be in front of him. He worked his way through grasses and brush but was unable to cross many of the gullies he came to.

"Damn storm really dumped on us this time," he muttered. In places, the mud was deep and thick, and after two hours of not finding anything worth talking about, he turned back. The slightest flicker of flame caught his attention off to the west. "That's over by the twin creeks. I wonder how close I can get?"

He was able to negotiate his way through one arroyo but was stopped cold at the creek, and instead of trying to cross the wild water, he rode on the high ground to the south. The fire glow he'd seen grew into a large campfire when he was within half a mile. "I'll be damned," he muttered. "He's on this side of the creek. Not for long, though.'

He took his rifle out of its scabbard, made sure there was a round in the chamber, and rode to within a few hundred yards of the flames. No moon and Doolin's big fire lit the area, giving McAvoy an easy stalk.

"On foot from here," he muttered. With his horse tied off tight, he stayed as close to the line of willows as he could and moved up on the fire in time to see Brad Doolin mount his horse. It was a long shot to start with, and with no light except from the fire, Clint McAvoy did the best he could. Doolin howled when the 45-70 bullet took a chunk of his ear off.

He sunk his heels into the horse's ribs and rode as low as he could into the darkness. Doolin had his arms wrapped around the horse's neck with the saddle horn pressed deep into his belly. The horse was in a panic and plowed through one arroyo where the water was almost chest deep. It was that that brought the horse back to a walk as it climbed out of the water and deep mud. Doolin felt the blood rolling down his neck, felt the ragged edge where the ear flap should be, and cussed long and hard before letting reality set in.

Who was that? Did that farmer follow me? He had a continuing line of questions, his shoulder was bleeding again, and his ripped-up ear hurt like hell. The only thing he knew for sure was that someone tried to kill him, and he needed to get back to the Anderson ranch, kill that bastard and take his wife for his own. The thought that it might have been someone from the posse shooting him never entered his head.

Was it fever from the infection that limited his ability to think? Or just stupidity all along? Doolin's outlaw mind should have him in the saddle running for his life for some community that would have a doctor. He should never have ventured cross country through mountains that reached ten thousand feet high. Least of all, he should not be aching for some farmer's wife instead of fearing a posse riding hard to kill him.

McAvoy ran back for his horse and was on the chase, riding hard, pulling up just before riding into the deep gully. "Damn fool rode right into that churning water." McAvoy rode along the banks until he found a decent ford and crossed, trying to figure out which direction he should ride to cut the outlaw off. He decided the best bet would be to ride to the ranch in order to give Anderson another gun for protection. *I know he's hurt, but I don' know how bad. At least I heard him scream out in pain. Protect Silas and Beverly is better than chasing a man in the dark.*

Corcoran was flat on his back, looking at billions of stars and wondering just what kind of man it was they were chasing. *I've done this for several nights now, and I still don't understand this fool. He should have ridden north into Carlin and jumped a train east. He's just plain lost right now, has thousands of dollars with him, and can't spend it on nothing.* In his own way, Corcoran knew there were no answers. *There are as many reasons as there are stars for a man to turn outlaw and not one of the reasons is worth losing sleep over.*

Way off in the distance, maybe a couple of miles or more, he was sure he heard a gunshot. Murphy was ten feet from Corcoran and sat straight up. "Was that a gunshot?"

"I think it was, Murph. Just one. Out that way," he said, pointing almost due east. "As dark as tonight is, it wouldn't be a hunter. We need to pack up and get moving. We're not that many hours from daylight." He had to chuckle because he knew the sun had only been down for a couple of hours.

Murphy convinced him that it would be more than foolish to ride off in the black of night without any kind of goal. "We'll get some sleep, Corcoran, and ride out at first light. We're dry and warm right now." That was the convincing argument.

Shorty Evans was first up and had the fire going, and coffee boiling before anyone joined him. *That Corcoran's*

*been on my case from the minute I met him. Well, not today,
Mister. I'm just as good as any man on this ride.*

"Rain sure made that air sweet last night," Jake Oxford
said, stretching for the sky. "Coffee smells better, too."
The air was filled with the aroma of side meat frying and
coffee boiling.

"We'll be riding hard today, Shorty, so let's make sure
those packs are tied tight."

"I always tie 'em tight," he turned and growled at Jake.
"Don't be telling me how to tie a pack."

Oxford looked long and hard at the older deputy and
wondered what got into his craw. "Just sayin' we need to...
Aw to hell with it. You got a bug in your pants, spit it out."

"Don't much care for youngsters tellin' me what to do,
Oxford. You just take care of your own self."

"Knock it off, Evans," Corcoran said. "Get them packs
put together and let's ride."

The group was on the trail in short order and on the
valley floor within the hour. "We'd a made a mess of things
if we'd ridden into this creek last night," Corcoran smiled.
"Glad we didn't. Doolin must have come onto this creek,
too. Even if we can't see his prints, we'd be best following
it."

They found Doolin's hasty attempt at a camp about
five miles or so downstream. "Damn mess of a camp,"
Murphy said. "Everything's muddy and wet."

"I'll bet he got washed out," Corcoran laughed.

"Got something," Shorty Evans hollered. "Looks like a
bloody chunk of ear."

After checking it out, Corcoran sent everyone out to
search for anything they could find. "Look for fresh prints,
look for signs of someone else around besides Doolin. We
know what his boot prints look like. Somebody shot him

last night but didn't kill him. Let's find out who and what direction everyone rode out in."

Like spokes in a wheel, the five spread out from the smoldering campfire. It was Jake Oxford who found McAvoy's boot prints and the group followed them to where he had tethered his horse and ridden off. Evans found which way Doolin rode, and Murphy split the posse. "Shorty, you ride with me and Snider. Oxford, you ride with Corcoran. I think you're right, Corcoran. I'll wager we'll find ourselves on the same trail within an hour or so."

Corcoran and Jake Oxford followed Doolin's trail to where he plowed through the creek. "That man was in a hurry," Corcoran chuckled. "Water's still up a bit right now, but it had to have been deep last night. The trail to the creek almost looks like he's on a run-away but coming up out of the creek, the trail snakes through and around the brush." He let Oxford ride up alongside.

"What was that dust-up this morning?"

"Shorty's been kinda short-tempered the last few days," he said. "Not sure why. "All I said was we needed to make sure the packs were tied down good and tight."

"Guess he ain't much for bein' out like this," Corcoran said. "I'd rather be out like this all the time than be stuck in a town all day. Sheriff don't much like me always being on the chase," he chuckled, "but I sure do." Oxford chuckled along with him. He was thinking how Sheriff Acord always had he and Buford Lamb do all the chasing, so he didn't have to leave town.

"My friend Buford Lamb was raised on a ranch and always wanted to be a lawman. I was raised in town and always wanted to be a buckaroo. Look at this country we're riding through," Jake said, spreading his arms wide, taking in a great expanse of open prairie. "I could ride

through open range like this all day every day and still
want more."

"You thinking of giving up the badge?" Corcoran asked.
"You have the makings of a fine lawman, Oxford. You and
I might want to have a long talk a little later. I'd sure like
to talk you out of that idea."

"Well, we can talk about it," Jake chuckled, "but if
the right offer came down the line, I'd trade this tin
badge for a good horse, open range, and a long lasso
any day of the week. Do you know how many dead
people I've seen just on this one chase? I know
there's gonna be more, too, before we stop this
Doolin fool."

"I'm afraid there will be, Mr. Oxford. I do believe there
will be," Corcoran said. *I like this kid, and if he gives it up, it
will be a loss to Frank Acord for sure. He has the heart of a poet
and the strength of a bull. He would probably fit in fine on a big
ranch in a valley like this.*

Following the trail in fresh ground was easy, and
Murphy was proved right. Within five miles Jake spotted
the others coming through the brush their way.

He pointed them out to Corcoran who noticed that
Murphy and them were stopped. "Wonder what they've
found? Let's ride over." The half-mile ride was quick, and
Murphy knew they were coming.

"Saw you out there and was about to try to get your
attention when this trail took a big turn to the south,"
Murphy said.

"Yeah," Corcoran yelled out. "Wondered why you
stopped. Doolin's trail keeps going, but I see this one
doesn't. Got any ideas?"

"It was pitch dark, and the shooter probably didn't
know his man was that close. There must be a ranch or

something close by, that way," Murphy said, pointing in the direction McAvoy rode.

"Let's check on the people at the ranch first," Corcoran said. "Killin' Doolin can come later. If it's Anderson's place, he might need some help."

CHAPTER FOURTEEN

McAvoy made the short ride back to the ranch and put his horse up. Silas Anderson heard him ride in and met him in the barn. McAvoy had mud on his boots and pants, and Silas noticed the horse had mud high on his legs. "Find anything?"

"I did, and I didn't finish the job." McAvoy was an angry man and told about the campfire, finding Doolin ready to ride off and shooting him. "I hit him, but he rode like a mad man into the deep night, Silas. I can pick up the trail at first light. Until then let's get this place set up for a good defense. There wouldn't have been any reason for him riding out late like that except to attack you."

"Now, he's got two wounds and a great desire for my wife. Bring your weapons and ammunition to the house, and we'll get set up. Looks like we'll be able to use those window slits I put in because of Indians that never attacked," he chuckled.

McAvoy set up at the front window to the left of the door while Beverly got the stove re-lit and coffee boiling. Anderson took the back window in the bedroom. The heavy wooden shutters were closed and braced, and only the thin gun slits allowed the men to see out. Beverly fried a platter of side meat and baked a basket of biscuits.

"You keep us in food and coffee, and we'll keep you safe and warm." McAvoy chuckled, spreading warm butter on a biscuit. Beverly felt a shiver go through her body, thinking about Doolin being out there.

"He must be a friend, Silas. Why would he come back here if he knows he's not welcome? Why wouldn't he just ride off? I'm a pretty tough old gal. Si, you know that, but I'm afraid."

Anderson took her in his arms and held her tight. "I won't let any man hurt you, sweetheart, I promise. Your folks didn't want us to be together because I have such a quick and mean temper, and because I'm so big and strong" he said, lifting her right off the floor. "But you know how much I love you.

"I do have a quick temper, but it's aimed at bad people and bad things."

"Like at the gate when it won't latch, and you tear it right off the hinges," she laughed. She felt the fear drain away as he squeezed her tight. His muscles were slabs of granite, and she knew she would be safe. She loved those muscles, took great pleasure is asking him to lift heavy objects just so she could see them. She'd run her fingers over them at night while in bed with him.

It was the accident with the calf that took its toll on their marriage. The calf twisted and drove its young horn deep into Silas Anderson's groin and it was only the quick response from her that kept him from bleeding to death. The accident made it impossible for them to have children, or for Anderson to be a complete man.

It was a long wait not knowing if there really would be

an attack. If Doolin comes will it be from the front or the back? What if he burns the barns instead of a direct attack? What if he tries to burn the cabin?

Silas Anderson ran the questions through his head so many times, and he was sure there would be at least one answer coming. It was just coming light, and Anderson couldn't sit and wait another minute. He stomped around the house and finally decided to take a walk outside.

"Stay back in the shadows, Clint, and keep those hawk eyes of yours wide open. Kill anything that moves." Beverly moved to the front window while McAvoy moved to the open door at the back to watch. Anderson bent low and moved fast across the open barnyard, ducking between fence lines, wagons, and sheds, working his way around the area close to the house.

He then moved out away from the open yard and worked his way back around through heavy brush and trees. He was back at the door within half an hour and inside. "Not a sign of any kind, and after that rain yesterday, any kind of man sign would stand out like a... a sign," he chuckled.

The long boring morning wore on with nothing being seen or heard. Beverly was about to put together some dinner for the boys when McAvoy yelled out, "Visitors. Looks like five mounted men riding in slow." McAvoy brought his rifle up and took aim on the lead rider, following him all the way in.

Anderson walked to the door and removed the brace. He handed the shotgun to Beverly and nodded to McAvoy. "Cover me." He stepped slowly onto the porch with his rifle cradled and ready. McAvoy was at the window slit, and Beverly was in the shadows of the open door. The riders pulled to a stop a good twenty-five yards out from the porch.

"Anderson, this is Deputy Sheriff Terrence Corcoran. Looking for a killer." He yelled it out, waving a hello at the house.

"Ride in and step down, Corcoran. Good to see you," Anderson yelled back. He turned and nodded to the cabin and stepped off the porch. "Might have met your killer yesterday," he said. "Black hair and beard, gunshot bad, and nasty temper. Said he was riding to Eureka to be a deputy, Corcoran."

Corcoran laughed right out. "He's riding from Eureka so as not to meet this deputy. Robbed a bank, killed two lawmen and others. You must have had a gun on him from the start, Anderson."

"Did," he said. "Coffee's on, got some food hot. Come on in we'll tell our stories. Beverly's some upset that this man had his eyes all over her, but she'll be glad to see you, Terrence."

Corcoran was a born flirt, and there were few women in Eureka County, married or not, who hadn't been flirted with by the man. They loved it; the husbands barely tolerated it. "Ah, dear Beverly," Corcoran said. "It's a good thing you put your brand on that lovely lady before I met her. She still the best cook in the county?"

Silas chuckled and nodded, shaking hands with the big deputy. "It's a good thing I know you're a gentleman, Corcoran. Bring your troops in."

"Put the horses in the barn, Oxford," Murphy said, "and climb up so you can see all around the property. Don't want that fool sneakin' in on us."

"Naw," McAvoy said. "You go on in with the others and have some coffee. I'll take the barn."

Corcoran introduced everyone as they found chairs around the kitchen table. Beverly brought the coffee pot over along with a platter of biscuits, warm butter, and fresh berry jam. Anderson brought a jug out from a cabinet. "I'm glad you're here, Terrence," she said, giving him a big smile. "That man frightened me. Silas wanted to shoot him, and it was I who said no. Clint is sure he's coming back." Corcoran smiled and grabbed a biscuit.

"That you what shot the man?" Giles Murphy asked Anderson.

"No. It was Clint McAvoy. Clint said Doolin was ready to ride from his camp late last night when he found him, and the shot spooked his horse bad. Had a full runaway until he hit a rain-swollen creek. Didn't follow him through that mess."

"He almost had him when he turned back to the ranch," Corcoran said. "McAvoy might be glad to know he blew one of his ears off."

Anderson had to smile at that. "I'll be glad to tell him that." He was standing at the window slit. "Doolin might not know you boys are here. You got plans, Corcoran?"

"I think right now is the best time to make those plans, eh Murphy?"

"Jake Oxford's been on Doolin's trail since the bank robbery in Winnemucca and is just about worn out. Why don't we leave him here with the Andersons and McAvoy? Give them one more gun and the rest of us will get on Doolin's trail. I want that fool dead or in irons."

Murphy looked around the table and caught himself. "I forgot, Snider. That wound of yours gettin' better? Can you ride with us or would you rather stay here."

"I can ride and fight, Sheriff. I'll ride with you."

"That good with you, Anderson?" Corcoran asked.

"The four of you should be able to hold him off if we don't catch him first." Anderson got a nod from Beverly and gave one to Corcoran. "Good. Let's ride," Corcoran said. "We'll ride him down and be back for supper." He chuckled, giving Beverly a little wink. She blushed and turned back to her stove, hoping no one saw.

Doolin rode along the bank of the creek for a short time and then turned away and rode through the brush and underbrush for the next two hours, finally stopping at a grove of pines. He wanted a fire bad but knew that would draw whoever it was that shot him, and simply tied off his horse, wrapped himself in a blanket, and slept. It was full daylight when he woke up, crying out in pain when he rolled onto what was left of his torn-up ear.

He climbed out from the blanket and quickly looked around, trying to get an idea of where he was and if he was alone. The long wide valley seemed to be flat as a hot cake, was empty to the eye and Doolin felt safe for the time being, but there was someone out there. Someone shot him last night. Someone chased him last night. "Who are you?" He shouted it out and didn't expect an answer.

All he saw were a few heads of cattle eating their way through good grass and brush, a few antelope spending time looking at him, and clouds building in the mountains to the west. There was the slightest breeze and virtually no sound. Doolin should be planning how to get out of this valley and away from the posse he must know was chasing him.

Scraping the wounded ear with the rough edges of the blanket opened it up, and blood spilled down his neck. He found some rags in a saddle bag and tried to stop the bleeding, crying out from the pain. "Dirty bastard," he muttered. "I'll kill that big farmer, and his woman will be mine," he said.

"To hell with all of you," he screamed at the open prairie and gathered wood from the trees to get a fire started. It would be a hot day again, but he needed a fire. A fire, out like he was, would be a form of security, and he needed that far more than he needed the warmth. He sat in the shade of the trees and worked out where he was, where the Anderson ranch was, and what he was going to do.

His saddle bags were strapped to the horse when he was chased off, so he had some food, he had the bank money, but none of the extras, like blankets, extra ammunition, extra food. "I got no choice, now," he muttered. "I gotta kill that man, take his woman, and make up a real pack to get me to Ward. Was it that big man that shot me last night? He's gonna die a long hard death."

He spent an hour trying to clean and cover his wounds, stomped out the fire, and made for the Anderson ranch. "Can't be more than five miles," he said, riding toward a slight rise in the valley for a better view. "That woman's gonna feel good. What's gonna feel real good is killin' that bastard farmer. Nobody shoots my ear off," he screamed at the empty valley.

He topped the little rise and saw smoke some seven or eight miles out and made for it. "I'll make her tend my wounds first." His shoulder was still bleeding from the effort to race away in the night, and his ear hadn't stopped bleeding since he scraped it open in the morning. He smiled thinking about her tender fingers working so carefully on him, and he spurred his horse into a gentle lope toward that column of smoke, still miles in front of him.

He remembered the way the ranch was laid out, how the cabin sat, with the door and one window, how the only safe way to ride up to the ranch would be to come from behind the big barn. Was there a door and window on the back of the cabin? He didn't know. "I gotta believe there is one, and I bet that woman is as good a shot as that bastard she's married to."

He had it all worked out as he neared the ranch. He had the horse back into a slow walk so he didn't kick up any dust and rode through as much brush as he could find, working toward the back of the barn. It was well past mid-day and shadows stood out, making the ride easier. When he was about two hundred yards from the barn, he spotted an arroyo that he could slip into.

With the horse tied to some brush in the muddy ditch, Doolin had his rifle and climbed to the rim to get a good view of the barn. There was no movement around any of the buildings, but a small column of smoke continued to drift from the main cabin. Doolin snaked his way through sage and rabbitbrush toward the back of the barn, his eyes darting in every direction hoping to spot whatever danger was waiting for him.

The barn was big enough to have an upper-level hayloft, had two stalls below, room to shoe the horses, and plenty of room for tack and equipment. The stairs up to the loft were as steep as a ladder, but wide windows at either end offered views of the valley north and south.

Doolin had gotten very close, maybe fifty yards from the barn, when he spotted a glint, a brief movement, near the barn doors. He burrowed down into the dirt, crawled slowly under a large sage, and watched for more move-ment. "That had to be a gun," he muttered. "They're waitin' for me. Bastards. She ain't gonna like what I got in store for her. Her, all soft and pretty, waiting to kill me?

"I'll give you something to think about, woman." He snickered and tried to see just who was waiting, and how he could get close enough to kill.

Anderson watched Corcoran and the posse ride off and called McAvoy in from the barn. "We gotta work this out, Clint. The barn and cabin are vulnerable to attack, but it's only one man doing the attacking. It ain't a bunch of howling Indians or a whole gang of outlaws. It's just one man, and there are four of us with guns."

"That one man's a mean one, Silas. We don't want to write him off. He's a sadistic killer even if he is badly wounded. Dangerous. I heard someone describe a man like that, one time. Called him a fiend." McAvoy opened the door to the cabin, and they joined Jake Oxford and Beverly.

"Me and Beverly can take care of the house, and you and Jake here keep the barn safe," Anderson said. "Two at each place and that outlaw will know what it means to threaten us," he chuckled.

"It'll be gettin' late soon," McAvoy said. "That's when he'll make a move. If he's still around, that is. Hell, he might have bled to death for all we know."

"Might of," Anderson said, "but we gotta believe he's alive and looking to kill us. How you feeling, Jake?"

"I'm fine, Mr. Anderson. It's been a long bunch of days, chasing this fella, but he killed my best friend, Deputy Buford Lamb. I got a score to settle with that boy, sir. He killed Pete Simpson, Sheriff Giles Murphy's deputy, too. No, sir, I'm just fine." He had a kind of crooked grin on his young face, and McAvoy knew that young lawman would stand up fine in a good firefight.

"All right, then," Anderson said. "What do you two need out there?"

"I got a good cache of food. There it's easy to get water," McAvoy said. "You got your bedroll and stuff with your horse, Jake?"

"Everything I'll need. Rifle, pistol, some jerky, bedroll, and ammunition. How will we know what's going on here at the house, Mr. Anderson?"

"Damned if I know, son. I know if I was gonna attack this ranch I'd come from behind the barn to do it. Ain't got no side windows on this old cabin. Can't see the barn from those gun slits, neither. You fight him off from there, and we'll fight him off from here," he chuckled, cuffing Oxford lightly on the shoulder.

That's funny, Jake thought. *He's calling me son, and I'm calling him sir, and we're about the same age, I think. Well, with a pretty little wife like that, I'll fight hard to keep them safe. He's about as strong a man as I can recall seeing.*

"He'll be comin' from that north end, Jake. You can bet on that. He'd be shielded from the house and be able to get close to the house without being seen. Silas and Beverly can just barely see the south doors of the barn, so we need to be watching north. I'll stay down here by the doors, and you go up on the hay rack."

The first two hours slipped by, dotted with occasional short conversations when Jake Oxford hollered down, "Got some dust out a mile or so, Clint. Ain't a dust devil for sure."

"Keep me posted. I can't see it from here." McAvoy smiled hoping that Doolin fool would ride right up and this time, he'd take his entire head off.

CHAPTER FIFTEEN

Corcoran found Doolin's tracks from the night before with ease, and they followed up to where he made his camp. "Easy to follow a man when he doesn't know where he is or where he's goin', Murphy. When he left here, though, he knows where he's goin'. Straight for Anderson's ranch."

Murphy and Aaron Snider rode to where Corcoran and Shorty Evans were looking at Doolin's tracks leading south toward Anderson's. "He got shot last night and doesn't seem to think anyone would be on his trail today? He's a bigger fool than I thought. Those people are in trouble, so let's ride."

Following fresh tracks after that heavy thunderstorm was easy, and Doolin didn't try any tricks to throw his followers off. It was midsummer, and there wasn't the slightest breeze, but way off to the west, thunderheads were building. The men had been in bad ones before, and they were not the least worried.

"Top that rise up there, and we should see the ranch," Corcoran said. "Time to get serious in our approach. Sure don't want to ride down on that fool and get another one of us shot up. Let's spread out, Murphy. Maybe a couple of hundred yards apart and walk our horses up to the ranch nice and slow."

"My first thought is to ride in hell for leather, Corcoran, but I know you're right. Thing that bothers me most is why Doolin ain't high tailin' it as fast as Mercury. Why ain't he headed for parts unknown?"

"Outlaws don't think like real people, Murph." Corcoran was laughing, then got serious. "He's gotta have mental problems more than we can imagine. He's all banged up, probably not a clue to where he is, and scared. Ever seen a badger got himself cornered? Whooie! That's what we'll be facing when we catch up. Rank as a dead skunk and mean as a badger."

"That's a nasty picture you just laid out, Mr. Corcoran." Murphy pulled his horse up and studied the valley between where they were and where the smoke indicated the ranch. "That cabin and barn are just specks so it's unlikely that we can be seen. Even less so if we're spread out and not riding all jammed up."

Mostly flat with gulches and arroyos here and there, stands of brush and stunted trees dotted the flats, and the ranch stood as a solitary object. "You can see that barn for miles, Corcoran. That's where he'll hit first. Probably try to burn it out, too, the bastard." He stood up in the stirrups looking out as far as possible.

"Shorty, ride out a half mile to my right and Snider, get between me and Shorty. Corcoran, ride out a few hundred yards to my left, and we'll ride at a walk. Nice and slow, no dust, and keep your eyes open."

"Let's not forget that Anderson is expecting an attack

and may not recognize us. Be prepared for that, too," Corcoran said.

The day was hot and humid as the rain from the day before evaporated and Corcoran watched more massive thunder clouds build over the mountains to the west. They were in for another set of thundershowers for sure, and probably within the next few hours. Cattle were scattered about on the open plain and didn't give much attention to the spread out riders. A few antelope shied away, and a gentle breeze came up that made the ride almost pleasant.

Wouldn't be hard to live in this country. I wonder if Mr. Oxford might have the right idea. Tuck this old tin badge away and find me a section of land in a valley like this, find me a pretty little redhead with a rank old sense of humor, and sit on the porch smokin' a pipe. Corcoran had to chuckle, riding slow and easy through the open valley. *Hell, I'd get the wandering bug every spring. I'm gonna stick to chasin' bad guys mainly because I get to wander into and through country like this. Sure, I'm riding a killer to ground, gonna see to it this fool, Doolin, pays the price, but, by damn, I'm gonna enjoy the ride. Jake Oxford has a different outlook on life than I do. Neither one of us is wrong, though.*

"Doolin has to hit the ranch, Murph," Corcoran yelled over to the Lander County Sheriff. "He lost so much when he was chased out of that camp, probably lost more from the flash flood. He doesn't have anything with him. He has to hit that ranch."

"That makes all the more sense for us to ride hell for leather, Corcoran, but I still know we can't. I know that young Humboldt County deputy has what it takes, and I'd make a bet on McAvoy. What about Anderson? Will he stand up to that fool?"

"With Beverly at risk? Oh, yeah, Murph. He'll do just

fine." *Except for the fact that Anderson can't control his temper, she would have a hard time finding a better husband. She's a long tall beauty, and he'll protect her for sure.* He couldn't control the smile those thoughts brought.

Everyone was tensed, eyes darting about, hoping to spot trouble before it spotted them as they rode toward the Anderson ranch. The tracks were written in large letters, they knew Doolin was in front somewhere, and killin' was on his mind. There was a breeze starting to blow, the clouds gathered and grew, and the riders all checked their weapons one more time riding across the broad valley.

"We need to turn more to the west, Murphy," Corcoran said. "We're coming straight in and might run into some rifle shots from that barn. Let's come in from an angle." Murphy agreed and moved the posse to the west about five hundred yards or so.

Doolin crept through the brush keeping as close to the ground as possible. He hadn't seen another glint or movement until he was about fifty yards from the wide barn doors. Just a hint of shadow moved, he thought. *Is that a man's shadow or just a damn animal in there. Don't want to shoot if it ain't a man. Gotta get closer.*

Jake saw a man start to move from under a sagebrush and brought his rifle up, took a long sight, and squeezed the trigger. "Damn," he said, seeing Doolin jump to his feet and race toward a wagon well off to the east of the barn doors. His shot blasted a limb from the sage Doolin was under, deflecting it away from the outlaw.

Oxford levered another round and fired just as Doolin dived under the wagon. "I missed with both shots, Clint. He's under that wagon," Oxford yelled down.

His face was bleeding from the shredded brush that was blown into it, but Doolin could see well enough to race behind the big hay wagon. He rolled behind one of the large wheels, saw Oxford in that upper window and took a quick shot, knocking wood splinters into Jake's face. He rolled toward the other end of the wagon, out of sight of the barn doors or upper window.

"If that big rancher is holed up in the barn that might mean that pretty little wife of his is waiting for me in the house," Doolin snickered. He wrenched his shoulder diving under the wagon and the pain seared. He knew the bandage would be wet with blood. He could feel the wound bleeding, his ear was bleeding, and he had bloody scratches across his face.

"You're gonna make me feel much better, little lady," he growled, easing his way to the end of the wagon and looking across the broad farmyard to the house. "That's a blank wall, no windows, and two fruit trees between me and the house."

McAvoy knew Oxford was okay and yelled up for him to stay put. He ran to the other end of the barn and tried to see out toward where that wagon was. He was also looking at the blank wall of the house and the two fruit trees. *Doolin doesn't know about me or Jake. Bet he thinks those shots came from Mr. Anderson.* He got as far outside the doors of the barn as he dared, but couldn't quite see the wagon.

"Shooting at the barn," Silas Anderson yelled back at Beverly. He was at the front door of the cabin and ran out onto the porch so he could look around toward the barn. Beverly yelled, tried to stop him, but he kept right on. Luckily, Doolin couldn't see him from under the wagon.

Anderson saw Clint McAvoy move as far out the barn door as he could and waved frantically at him, finally catching his attention.

McAvoy used his hands and arms to give Anderson an idea of where Doolin was, and Anderson signaled back that the two should move on Doolin. McAvoy put his hands up to say "Not yet," and ran into the barn. "Come on down, Jake. I think we have that bastard in a trap." He ran back out to the front of the barn and waved at Anderson.

Doolin saw them coming well before they knew exactly where he was and, staying as low as possible, rolled and crawled back through the heavy brush. He worked his way to his horse and mounted up, riding east at a hard run. It was the posse's move to the west that kept them from riding up on Doolin's tied off horse.

"So, Mr. big rancher, you have help, eh? That ain't gonna save that pretty little wife of yours." He was laughing riding into a muddy swale that held a stream flowing from the eastern mountains. He climbed off his horse and knelt in the stream, washing his face. There was lots of blood from the shattered sagebrush. He filled his canteen, mounted up, and rode toward the eastern foothills of the next range.

Using hand signals, Anderson was able to cover and move McAvoy and Oxford as they worked their way to the wagon only to find no one there. Some blood on the ground and indications of someone crawling away was all they found. "He must have spotted us and hightailed it," Silas said as they slowly followed the trail to where the horse had been.

"I was sure we'd have him this time," Clint McAvoy said.

"I don't know how that first shot of mine missed him," Jake said. "I had dead aim on his head."

"Blew up a sagebrush right in front of him, Jake. Probably sent your bullet just off enough to miss. Let's get Beverly to fix up that pretty face of yours, shall we?" Jake blushed some but followed Anderson and McAvoy toward the cabin.

The posse wasn't half a mile from the barn when they heard the rifle shots. "Let's go," Corcoran shouted, putting the spurs to Rube. The four men slowly closed ranks as they raced through the brush, grass, and stunted trees. They rode hard to the front of the house where the three men were standing.

"Get him?" Corcoran, the first one in, yelled, pulling Rube to sliding stop.

"He got away somehow," Jake yelled back. "He must have spotted us comin' up on him and ran off. His trail is plain out in the brush behind the barn."

"Stay with Anderson, then," Corcoran yelled, signaled the posse to follow him, and jumped back in the saddle for the chase. Doolin's trail stood out in the open plain, and the posse followed the fresh prints at a lope. "Watch for an ambush, but let's ride that bastard down, Murphy. This guy's name should have something to do with cats. I've never seen a man able to evade us every time we get close. Nine lives? He's on his last one now."

Doolin must have had a feeling that he would be followed this time and put his horse in a hard run, riding toward some jagged rocks standing above a copse of aspen trees. "Must be water near there and maybe I can lose those fellers in the rocks. Or let 'em get close enough to kill 'em. Gonna kill that rancher long and slow, I am."

It was a hard ride through the aspens, and he let his horse make its way through the tangle of rocks, getting high onto a ridge line that he figured he could hide behind. The pain in his shoulder was even worse than when he rolled under the wagon. His face was bleeding again as was his ear.

He rode between two rocky spires across the low end of the ridge and turned uphill, toward a stand of pine and cottonwood. "There's the water," he said, jumping off his horse near a large pine tree. He tied off quickly and ran to the edge of the sawtooth ridge.

"There you are," he whispered, crawling over behind a large rock outcrop. He was looking down the steep and rocky slope at the four men coming slowly at him. "Come on, boys, I got a surprise for you." He had his rifle cradled to his good shoulder and watched Corcoran lead the four riders up through a tangle of rocks. *There's four of 'em. Where'd those others come from?*

"Time to go on foot, Murph. He could be behind any of those rocks, trees, or bushes."

"Don't want to but you're right. Snider, take care of the horses and rewrap that wound. You're bleedin' again. Let's go."

Doolin watched as three men slowly made their way up the hillside. They were still well out of rifle range and didn't know where he was. "No," he muttered. "Time to get back to that ranch before it gets dark. If her man and hired help are out here, it means she's alone." He chuckled. "Waiting for me."

He crawled back to his horse through tumbled rocks, boulders, and scree, untied the horse, and walked toward the other end of the ridge. He tried to be as quiet as possible moving through the rocks. It was at least a half mile before he dropped over the side and made his way on foot down to the valley floor.

He was in the saddle and on his way to the ranch before Corcoran and the posse cleared the ridge. Corcoran was well versed in tracking outlaws in the great Nevada desert and called Shorty Evans over. "See how a rock here and there seems out of place? See how some are turned over, wet side up? This is how you track a man through rocks."

"Yeah," Evans said, "Murphy's told me about that. So?"

"So? It means we're gonna need our horses. He's been walking his horse away from us all the while we worried about him settin' up an ambush. Run back and bring them and Snider back with you. Murphy and I will continue tracking this fool." *For an older man wearing a badge, Evans ain't the smartest I've had to work with. He's the kind that'll get you killed fast.*

"Murph," Corcoran yelled back to the Sheriff. "Stay alongside or behind, not in front of me, and we'll run him down. He's making for the south end of this ridge."

Doolin was far more interested in speed than deception, and Corcoran and Murphy made good time walking the length of that ridgeline. Shorty and Snider joined them at about the halfway mark. "He's looking to get back in the valley, Murph. He's gonna find a place to wait for late night and hit that cabin. We need to get back there."

Following Doolin's trail was again easy once they reached the valley floor and it was obvious Doolin was riding to the ranch. "You got a plan, Murphy?"

"Only one. Hang the bastard," Murphy quipped. "You?"

"I'm thinkin'," Corcoran laughed. "We could send

Snider ahead to warn Anderson and get that wound looked to, and we could ride Doolin down. Might get lucky and get to him before it gets dark. Snider could take a straight line to the ranch."

"Might could do that, but those thunder clouds are gonna get us first," Murphy said, pointing at the massive boomers working their way across the valley. 'Coming right at us, again, I do believe. Sending Snider off, though, is a good idea."

He called the young deputy over, told him the plan, and watched him ride off toward the Anderson ranch. "He's been a good deputy, Corcoran. Learns fast and ain't afraid of nothin'."

Corcoran caught the sneer that crossed Shorty Evans' face at the comment. They rode Doolin's trail across the open plain, up swales and down through gulches, around outcrops and always toward the ranch. The thunder was getting louder, and lightning strikes were more than visible. It was late in the afternoon as they approached a stand of scrub pines, and Corcoran said it would be best to huddle up there until the storm is over.

"Doolin won't ride through this, either," Murphy said. "Spread the tarp and get a fire going while we can. Keep the pack as dry as possible. At least we can drink some coffee and do some plannin'. Snider's gonna be one wet puppy when he gets to the ranch."

Doolin couldn't see the ranch when the first cold raindrops began to pelt him. The wind was beginning to get serious, and bolts of lightning followed by tremendous thunderclaps bounced off the desert floor, driving him toward some cottonwood trees. He dismounted under a large one and noticed it was along the banks of an arroyo. He got back in the saddle, rode across the gulch and dismounted several hundred yards from the drainage. Using his horse as an anchor, he spread his bedroll and sat in the dirt, under it.

Bit once, Doolin wasn't going to get bit again. Midsummer thunderstorms in the high mountain deserts of Nevada are often filled with hail and freezing rain, and it wasn't long before Doolin's teeth were chattering. "Should have stayed under those trees and made a fire," he snarled. The rain, lightning, and thunder were incessant, and Doolin's bedroll was drenched and heavy when he said, "to hell with it," and climbed back in the saddle.

He hadn't gone ten feet when he saw a massive bolt of lightning hit one of the cottonwood trees, blasting it into a million pieces. "Damn," he whispered and hunkered down in the saddle, urging the horse into a trot.

Visibility was poor at best, and he feared he would ride up too close to the ranch. He spotted another stand of trees, debated for only a few seconds, and rode toward them to sit out the storm. The trees gave limited protection, and he simply sat down on a rock to wait it out. His mind though, offered pictures of Beverly Anderson, in bed, waiting for him. Was he mad? He knew the posse had to be charging down on him. Was it the pain from his shoulder, his ear, that kept him moving toward her, not seeking safety?

Outlaws come in many shades of stupid, and Brad Doolin had to be close to the head of the pack. He dismissed the idea of simply riding east, away from danger. He wasn't thinking about killing Anderson so he could bunker up and fight the posse. He was only thinking of the carnal pleasure of Anderson's wife. Maybe he was simply a stupid, mad man.

He watched the storm move across the wide valley, felt the winds and rain ease up and moved out from the trees. "I'm gonna sleep in that big man's warm bed with that pretty girl in my arms tonight," he muttered, stepping into the saddle. He needed to find some place to hide until dark, someplace where he could dry off.

"Damn, I want a fire," he said. The ground was muddy, deep pools of water hid deep arroyos, and his ride was slow as he made his way to Anderson's. "There was a rock outcrop about half a mile from the cabin, I think. I'll get behind that and get dry and wait."

Snider was several hundred yards from the cabin and knew he might get shot if he didn't approach nice and slow. He needed for them to know he was coming in peaceful once they spotted him. He put his horse in a trot and came toward the cabin in a zigzag, making as much dust as he could in the still damp ground. The new storm was so close the thunder hurt his ears, but the rain hadn't started yet.

"Single rider coming in," Jake Oxford yelled from the front window. "Looks like he wants us to know he's comin'."

Anderson had his rifle, Beverly had the shotgun, and Clint was at the window. "Cover me," Anderson said and stepped out onto the porch. "Looks like one of the posse members."

Oxford yelled out, "That's Aaron Snider. Hope he's not hurt more. He got nicked when Doolin was sprung."

Anderson waved the deputy in. "I'll take care of his

horse, Oxford. Find out why he's here, and the rest aren't. Bolt that door 'till I get back."

Beverly sat Snider at the table and started work on his wound right away. "Why'd they send you back, Aaron?" Oxford asked.

Murphy and Corcoran folded the tarp while Shorty saddled the horses. "We'll have to watch for arroyos, Murph. Standing water will hide them. Damn dangerous."

"I tried to be a rancher once, Corcoran. I know these valleys and the danger. Lost cattle in flash floods every year. Damn quicksand catches you. Think we'll make the ranch before dark?"

"Depends on those flash floods you were talking about," Corcoran chuckled. "Fording a fast running drainage gulch can get mighty spooky. Knee deep mud, quicksand, fast water. Everything designed to kill you. Damn dangerous."

Those were prophetic words as Corcoran was soon to find out. They rode past a still smoldering cottonwood tree and found where Doolin hid under his bedroll. "He stopped out here and then went across the stream before it became this raging flood," he said as the group rode up to the arroyo Doolin had crossed. "We gotta find a ford and soon. Shorty, you go upstream, and Murphy and I will go down. Fire off a shot if you find a good crossing."

Shorty Evans grumbled some and turned his horse upstream at a trot. *It's always me that gets sent out to do something. Go saddle the horses. Go find a ford.* He didn't give a thought that the folks at the cabin were in mortal danger because Doolin was riding toward them. Evans was about half a mile out and found a wide spot in the gulch. Would it simply be soft, deep mud or would it be sand and gravel? Quicksand was always possible, and Shorty slowly walked his horse into the stream. The bottom was good and solid; the water was fast and cold. Shorty was a good rider, stayed in the saddle as water was up to the horse's belly, and he lunged the horse across with no problem. One shot from his revolver brought the other two at a run.

"We're gonna run out of daylight before we get to the ranch, Corcoran." Murphy urged the group into a lope. "Probably this rain washed out Doolin's tracks too," he snarled. They rode up and over a rise in the valley floor and could see smoke from the Anderson ranch, many miles away.

"You got a plan, Corcoran?"

"Not really," he said. "Best if we don't just ride in, though. We want to catch or kill Doolin, not chase him off again. He's been mighty slippery so far. When we get close enough to see the building good, we should probably dismount and walk in slow and quiet."

They rode up to within a few hundred yards of the ranch and tied their horses in a stand of pines at the bottom of a swale. "See that rocky outcrop out to our left? It's a good thing it's out this far, out of rifle range of the house. Doolin could almost set up a siege from there, but it's too far out.

"Shorty, see if you can circle around and come up on that barn from the other side. Take your time and be quiet. It's gonna be mighty dark real soon." Corcoran looked at Murphy for his nod of approval. "Good. I'll swing way around to the south and come up on the cabin from the east side, and Murphy, you sneak straight in." Again, Murphy nodded his okay and Corcoran continued.

"We won't be able to communicate, so just play this by

ear. Make your own decisions, make your own play, but remember that the others are close. Let's not shoot each other." There weren't any chuckles or snickers, and the three stood out in the gathering dark of night. The clouds were gone, and stars made their presence known, but there was no moon to make getting through the prairie any easier.

"I got a better idea," Murphy said. "Shorty, you and I will come up on the cabin from the south side. Corcoran, you sneak around and come in through the barn from the north."

Corcoran cocked his head off to the side a bit and looked at Murphy. Murphy had his jaw set and motioned Shorty Evans to start walking toward the cabin. He whispered to Corcoran, "I don't want him off by himself. He'd surely do something to get us killed. I'll keep him with me."

The smell of wet sage following a summer storm is wonderful, and even the dust, as it gets wet offers a special aroma. None of this was being enjoyed as the three men slowly worked their way to the cabin. Doolin could be anywhere, might see them well before they saw him, and their fear might also be an aroma in this night air.

Doolin left his horse tied off in the outcrop and walked slowly toward the ranch house in the gathering gloom. Dusk falls fast in the high mountain deserts, light enough to see and then, within seconds, pitch black. Doolin had a good bead on the house and took his time, being careful not to trip or make a noise. He could see the house; they couldn't see him.

Light shone through the gun slits in the windows,

smoke from the house drifted east, and Doolin made good progress through the wet grass and brush. He knew he had to have a plan, tried to remember what the cabin looked like inside and knew there were at least two rooms, windows on both the east and west sides but not the north or south. "Yes," he murmured, "there was a door on that east side, too."

He stayed as low as he could as he got closer to the house and a plan slowly took hold. "Burn 'em out," he whispered. Making his way around the cabin and coming up from the east side, he could only see a dim light from the window slit. "They're in the front room of the house," he whispered as if talking to a companion. He wanted to creep up and look through that gun slit but fought off the notion.

I can get around to that barn, light it off, and when they run out to save their precious animals, kill the two men and have me a beautiful woman. The obsession with Beverly would drive his every move and thought as he continued his planning. He forgot that just a couple of hours ago he thought the men in the posse were Anderson and his hired men. Was it the fever from his infected shoulder that threw his thinking off?

"It's too early to attack," he muttered. "Gotta wait." He found a stand of pine trees about thirty yards back from the building and made his way. Stars were shining bright now but there wasn't any moon. He dug down into a bed of pine needles and laid down for a quick nap. "After midnight, pretty girl, you'll be mine, and big man farmer, you'll be dead." Sleep, dreams of Beverly, dreams of spending thousands of dollars, drifted through the hours.

CHAPTER SIXTEEN

"So the rest of the posse is chasing this Doolin feller, and Corcoran figures he's coming here." Anderson was sitting across from Snider at the kitchen table. "Well, we'll be ready for him, won't we. You've been riding hard for several days with those gunshot wounds. You gonna be up for a fight?"

"I've been looking for a fight with that man from the minute that bullet hit me," Snider growled. "Yeah, I'm up for a fight." He looked over at Beverly who was putting more wood in the fire. "Thank you," he said. "Whatever that stuff is you put on me, it works."

"Old Shoshone medicine my mother learned about many years ago. She and my father lived near the Shoshone when they were youngsters. Just ground up weeds is what most people call it, but it works," she laughed.

"Sure does," he said. Snider turned his attention back to Silas Anderson. "Corcoran thinks Doolin will attack late tonight. He's hurt bad, lost most of his camp in a thunderstorm, and probably doesn't have any food either."

"A cold and hungry man is like a cornered bear,"

Anderson mused. "Damn dangerous. He has a lust for my wife, and it will be my pleasure to kill the man." Anderson's anger at not killing him at that first encounter was still obvious. "I don't care how wet, cold, and hungry he is, I don't care if he's on his knees begging, I'm gonna kill him."

Beverly walked over to her husband and put a hand on his shoulder. "Save that temper of yours for the fight, Silas. I'm worried about our cabin. What if he tries to burn us out? We gotta save our cabin." She looked into his eyes and knew he would take on lions and tigers to protect her. "Is that thunder?"

"Old Doolin's gonna get wet again, then," Clint McAvoy laughed. "We got another big storm bearing down on us right now." The rumbling thunder could be heard and was coming closer by the minute, lightning could almost be felt it was so close, and now they could hear rain pelting the roof.

"He knows about me and Beverly, maybe knows you're here, too, Clint, but he doesn't know that Aaron Snider and Jake Oxford are here. We've got lots of big guns waiting for him," Anderson chuckled. "Beverly, why don't we eat soon, then two or three of us can sleep while the rest watch, then switch up." Anderson's anger for letting the man even come up to the house the first time, was one thing, but as he thought about it, he became even more angry from the aborted attack, and now, seething for a fight with Doolin.

"You need to calm yourself, Silas," Beverly said. "You've always said that going into a fight angry is a good way to lose the fight. We need you to be thinking, not reacting."

"Those are my words, Bev, and you're exactly right. Thank you. We need to think this out; be prepared for any attack." Anderson walked to the stove and gathered his lovely wife in his arms, kissed her forehead, and smiled. "I will control my anger, Bev. I will."

The brief and furious thunderstorm lashed the prairie while they ate bowls of hot stew, fresh biscuits, and a summer special of fresh peach cobbler for dessert. "You boys stay awake," McAvoy laughed. "I'm taking second watch. That's when he'll hit. Late, and I'm gonna be the one to punch some lead through his vile body." He stood up and stretched, yawned, and walked toward the back room.

The old buckaroo, McAvoy, stood up suddenly and turned. "If I was attacking this place, I'd start with burning the barn to draw us out." Clint McAvoy didn't like the idea of everyone bundled up in the house. Most of all he didn't like the idea of him being bundled up in the house. "We need a couple of us out at the barn and the rest in here."

"I agree with Clint," Jake Oxford said. "I think we would have a much better chance if half of us were at the barn. You, Silas, Snider, and Beverly, set up your defense here in the house and Clint and I can fight from the barn."

Silas thought about that for a short time and nodded. "Yeah, you're right. Sure wish I'd put windows on the north and south sides of this old house."

"He won't hit until after midnight," Oxford said. "He'll hope everyone will be sleeping and he'll attack."

Jake Oxford saw to it the wood stove was stoked and coffee was hot while Aaron Snider took up a position along the west wall near the window gun slit. The night was dark with heavy clouds, and he wasn't able to see a thing.

"Might be best to just have one candle burning," Jake

said. "Can't even see nothin' out there." He blew out the lamps that hung near the table and those mounted on the wall opposite the stove. "That's better. You set yourself up on that east window. You ready to head out to the barn, Clint?"

"Yup. You take the high perch to the north, and I'll take the high one to the south. Storm's over, but the clouds are still with us. Won't get much help from a moon or stars. Let's go nice and slow getting out there. It's possible he's watching."

Snider chuckled. "That barn is an open target that can't be seen from the house. I think if I was lookin' to attack this house, I'd do something to get these cabin doors open."

"Me, too," Oxford said. "Like set the barn on fire." He and McAvoy slipped out of the house through the front door and crept slowly out to the barn, using everything available to duck behind or under on their way. It had rained so hard in the two large thunderstorms that there was standing water they had to wade through.

Both men knew that a fire was out of the question and they would have to put up with wet feet for the next few hours. "Can you make the sound of an owl?" McAvoy asked.

"Sure can," Jake answered.

"Good. Two hoots means you see something, and I'll come running. Same from my end."

It was well after midnight when Snider woke Anderson up. "No action, yet," he said. "Stove is full of wood, and it's time for me to sleep some."

"Not seen anything, eh? Maybe he's bled to death,"

Anderson said. "That would be too good a death for the bastard. Get some sleep, and we'll take it from here."

Doolin wasn't aware of the changing of the guard in the house when he awakened and started to move about in the dark. A breeze was blowing, and the desert night was cold. "That burning barn will warm things up," he snickered. He slowly moved from under the trees and through open ground toward the barn.

"Damn," he said, looking back at the cabin when he was still a hundred feet or so from the barn's open doors. "They ain't no window in that house for them to see the fire. Hell, this thing could burn for an hour before they even knew it," he muttered. He worked his way back to the stand of trees. It was very dark, and he had trouble finding his way, doin his best not to stumble or make noise.

For the next hour, he sat under the trees trying to figure out how to get those two men to run from the house so he could shoot them. "Fire has to be the answer," he said. He made his way out and around to the south side of the house and moved up as close as he dared. "If I pile up some brush along that wall and in front of the door, and light it on fire, that wall will catch real easy. Old dry wood like that, and they'll scramble out the other door. They won't be able to get out the burning door but will need to get that fire out." He was on his haunches, quietly talking to himself, working out his plan.

Given half a chance sagebrush will burn even when it's sopping wet and one thing that is available in Nevada's high mountain deserts is sagebrush. He was cold, actually shivering, but probably more from fever than the breeze that was blowing. "I gotta burn this cabin now.

"But which door?" He said, standing up and looking

back and forth, east and west. His shoulder ached, and he wasn't able to move it easily from stiffness and cold. He tried to dismiss the pain, fought off pangs of hunger, but couldn't dodge the fear that was building. There were two men and a desirable woman inside that building with food, a warm fire, and safety, and he was out here in the damp, cold, hungry and hurting. The thought that he was running from a posse looking to kill him was supplanted by the visions he had of Beverly Anderson.

The idea that burning the cabin in order to shake out the defenders would leave him without a cabin also never entered his addled mind. He wanted to scream at them, shoot holes in that big blank wall he was staring at, and sat back down in the wet ground, rubbing the bloody bandage on his torn ear, trying to get his shoulder to move about some.

"Can't wait no more and can't burn that wall. Gotta make the fire at that front door. They can't come out there, and I'll be back up in those trees, waitin' for them to come out the back door."

He spent the next half hour quietly bringing as much brush and wood as he could to pile up at the front door of the cabin. No one inside heard any of that. He had the pile directly in front of the door and spread some to each side. He sprinkled a goodly amount of black powder around the base of his woodpile and struck a spark. He waited until he was sure it caught and moved as quickly as he could back to his nest and his trusty rifle. It took just moments for the sage to catch and soon there was an inferno blazing on that old wooden porch.

"All right, Mr. big rancher, you come out that door in a hurry and die. And your friend right behind you." Doolin sat quietly with only thoughts of Beverly dancing in his head, seeing the glare from the fire in the wet ground. Unpainted wood sitting in Nevada's summer suns for more than ten years burns hot and fast.

Corcoran was almost to the north end of the barn, maybe twenty-five feet or so from the closed doors when he heard an owl hoot twice. "If I was fightin' Indians tonight instead of chasing a bank robber, I'd say I'd just been spotted. It was a fair imitation, but that weren't no owl hootin' up in that barn." He murmured and chuckled.

"Is that hoot-owl Doolin? No, it can't be because he's alone, and that means it's one of ours, and that makes it bad for me. My old hoot-owl buddy doesn't know I'm one of the good guys." He chuckled softly again. "I need to let him know before he shoots me."

He was flat on the wet and muddy ground, snaking his way to a clump of brush when a rifle cracked, and a bullet came within an inch of his head. He rolled hard under the brush and pulled his revolver but didn't shoot. He decided to try and sneak one over on the shooter. *I know that ain't Doolin in there and I surely don't want to shoot one of our people.* He was in a fix and finally simply yelled it out.

He brought himself to a sitting position behind the brush and hollered out, "This is Deputy Sheriff Corcoran. You are surrounded. The game's over, Doolin. Throw down your weapons and come out of that barn. If I see a gun, you're a dead man." He chuckled again knowing the hoot-owl would chuckle too.

"You are one scary sumbitch, Corcoran, and I'm sure glad to hear your voice," Jake Oxford yelled down from the barn window. Come on in, won't you?" Oxford started down the steep steps, caught a heel, and tumbled the rest of the way. He landed on his left leg, and his knee turned the wrong way.

"Damn me, that hurts," he said, trying to get back on his feet. He grabbed a hay rake and used it to get up. He couldn't put any weight on his leg and had to limp using the rake as a crutch."

"Gonna be all right, boy?" McAvoy hollered out, coming down the steps at his end of the barn.

"Twisted my knee something fierce, Clint, but I'll live. Hope I don't have to chase nobody," he snickered.

"Sure glad you ain't no marksman, Jake," Corcoran said with a touch of wry to his comment. "Just damn near clipped me, you did. Hello, McAvoy," he said as Clint walked up to open the door. "Anybody else out here with you? We're spread out and around the cabin hoping to catch that fool before he does bad things."

"You're the only one we've seen," McAvoy said. "I better get back to that south door." He sauntered across the barn to the big doors, and Corcoran walked with him. Oxford muttered and cussed as he climbed back up to his north window perch.

"That was a rifle shot," Giles Murphy said. "Out near the barn, I think. Stay with me. We need to keep close watch on this side of the cabin." He and Shorty Evans were off a couple of hundred yards to the southeast of the cabin, tucked under some scrub cedar bushes. "Corcoran was heading for the barn. If there's more gunfire, we'll go."

"It's a black night, Sheriff, with all those clouds hanging around. I'm not sure we would see anyone moving around anyway, and I don't think we dare get closer to the house, either. Why would Doolin not just ride off? Corcoran was so sure he'd ride back here. What makes Corcoran the expert around here?"

"Don't much care for kind of talk, Shorty, and you know it. Corcoran's one of the best law dogs I've ever met. Now, with Doolin? He's hurt bad, Shorty. He's out of food, probably doesn't even have a full camp, either, and we're many miles from anywhere. He almost has to be here, and those people in that cabin are in danger."

"Woman or no woman, if it was me, I'd be heading in any direction than this one," Shorty said.

"That's because you're not an outlaw," Murphy laughed. "Let's go."

Inside the cabin, Silas Anderson jumped from the kitchen table when the rifle shot went off. "At the barn," he said. He raced to the door, and Snider stopped him. "We got to get out there."

"No!" Snider snarled, holding the angry man fast. "That might just be what he wants. You go racing out that door, and you'd run into a hail of bullets, Anderson. If there's more gunfire, we'll go slow and easy."

Anderson wanted to argue, wanted to race to the barn, and Snider's logic edged its way forward, and he slumped into a chair. Beverly walked over and put her hand on his shoulder, giving the big man a little squeeze. "I hate this, just sitting," he said. He reached up and patted her hand. "Waiting for him to attack us instead of us attacking him." Snider poured him a cup of coffee and got back to his window slot.

Murphy whacked Shorty Evans and pointed. "Cabin's on fire. Doolin's lit the cabin on fire to draw them out. Let's go." He and Evans raced down out of the trees toward the front of the cabin knowing someone might be at that window slit waiting to shoot. "Keep low and off to the side until we get there. Watch for Doolin, but he'll be guarding the other door."

"Why?" Evans asked. Murphy wanted to slap some sense into the man, but at the same time expected that kind of question from the unthinking deputy.

"He wants them to run out to put out the fire or get away from it. You gotta start thinking, Shorty. You'll get shot sure as hell if you don't." They were slogging through the mud, tripping over brush and ran as fast as they darted toward the cabin.

"Do you smell something?" Snider looked around the kitchen and Anderson jumped up, pointing at the front door. Smoke was pouring in the cracks and flames could be seen. "He's trying to burn us out," Snider said. He tried to open the door, but the heat and flames drove him back. Anderson made a break for the back door before Snider could stop him.

"Gotta get that fire out," Anderson yelled, slamming the bolt aside and pulling the back door open. He ran out into the cold night, one shot rang out, and Anderson was down and dead, a bullet in the middle of his chest. Beverly started for the door, screaming Anderson's name and Snider grabbed her before she reached the door, but it meant that he didn't have his rifle in hand nor could he grab his pistol.

Doolin slammed his way through the door that fast, knocking both of them back. He had his pistol in hand, shoved Snider aside as he fired, once, twice, and Snider was driven onto the floor, two bullets deep in his belly and out of the game. Doolin flung the squirming Beverly aside and pushed the door shut, ramming the bolt into place.

"Just you and me, little darlin'," he said, a horrible grin on his face. "Let's have some coffee and talk about all this." He pushed her toward the kitchen, keeping the revolver aimed at Snider, who wasn't moving. She could see blood all but running free from his shoulder wound.

She cringed back from the man. His face was covered in blood from the splintered sagebrush, one ear was mangled and a bloody mess, and his shoulder, partially covered in bloody rags smelled bad. Doolin had a fiendish grin on his face as he moved closer to her. His bad arm hanging loose, his other with a pistol in hand. Could she fight this madman off? How best to do that? And, what about Silas? Was he dead?

Oh, Silas, why? I need you. How can I fight this monster?

The kitchen was filled with smoke, and flames from the burning door were spreading onto the walls. The heat kept them from the stove and Doolin grabbed Beverly and shoved her into the back room. He had his good arm wrapped around her, and she was thrashing, screaming, kicking to no avail. The wall alongside the door was burning hot, and if Doolin had been thinking, he would have known that the roof would also soon catch fire.

"Sit down," he snarled, shoving her toward a chair near the north wall. She was sobbing, holding herself tight, and sunk into an old cane rocker. "We ain't gettin' no coffee, but I will be getting what I really want," he smirked. Doolin moved over to make sure Snider was dead, and Beverly rushed for the door.

Doolin jumped to his feet and slapped her hard with the rifle barrel, knocking her to the floor. "Next stupid move like that and I'll kill you, woman." He wanted her naked, in that bed over there, not cowering on the floor, bleeding all over that pretty dress she was wearing. But he couldn't have her running off, now, could he? "I really don't want to kill you, woman, but I will if you try something again."

She was sobbing and watched him reach over and try to rub his wounded shoulder, saw him grimace and almost cry out in pain. She averted her eyes when he quickly looked up to see if she was watching. "I need some of your loving doctoring, woman. My shoulder feels like it's going to fall right off."

"Medicine's in the other room. It's on the table, but I don't think you can get to it. I hope your shoulder rots off. You're a filthy murderer," she cried out.

He moved quickly to the doorway and saw the kitchen fully engulfed in flames. The heat drove him back to where she was trying to get to her feet. "You'll make me happy first, then make me well," he said. An evil laugh was followed by another blow to Beverly's head from the rifle barrel.

She flopped back onto the bed, and he stood over her, lust all but visible in his battered face. He slowly started to undress, changed his mind, and bent to unfasten her clothing. He only had one arm and hand in working order and cussed in a rage. He had to put the rifle down to get at the buttons holding her clothing. He screamed out his anger and desire, tearing at her bodice.

"You're mine, woman, and will be forever."

CHAPTER SEVENTEEN

"Throw that brush aside," Murphy yelled when he and shorty got to the house. They had just reached the porch when Murphy held up his hand. "Gunfire out back, just like I said. You go that way, and I'll run around from this side." Shorty Evans kicked as much brush as he could and raced around the north end of the house. The fire was well established, the door in flames and the wall above the rocks was already afire.

Flames were licking upward fast, moving onto the sod roof. It wouldn't be long, and the old structure would be falling down on itself. Murphy could hear sounds from inside, but the noise of the fire made it difficult for him to make sense of them.

Murphy slowed before rounding the edge of the building, using the wall for protection. He couldn't see anyone moving, and the door to the cabin was shut. He could still hear movement inside and moved out into the darkness. He stumbled over rocks and debris, and when he tripped on something soft, he leaned down to find Anderson's body, face down in the mud.

"Must have done exactly what Doolin wanted him to do. Sorry we weren't able to stop this from happening, old man," he muttered. Murphy slowly moved across the open area and closer to the back door of the house, keeping as far from the window gun slot as possible. He got as close to the door as he could, hoping he would be able to hear something.

All he got was muffled sounds. The door and walls were made of heavy timbers that would withstand bullets and high winds, but not fire. "If Anderson ran out, that means that Snider is still inside," he grumbled. What he wanted to do is ram his body through that door, guns blazing. Maybe kick the door into shreds then shoot Doolin fifteen times.

Murphy was also a logical man and knew the proper thing to do was wait for the rest of the posse to join him. "Then we'll all kick that damn door in." He had to snicker wishing that they could do that. "With Beverly and Snider in there, we will have to be more patient than I want to be and far more careful than I usually am." The murmuring continued as he stood near the door, hearing movement from inside. *Where's Corcoran and the others? Where's Shorty, damn it.*

"He's lit the front of the house," McAvoy cried out, seeing the flames from the piled up brush. "Let's go." He and Corcoran ran from the barn and were almost to the house when they heard the rifle shot. It was just moments later they heard two pistol shots from the back of the cabin.

Corcoran's long legs carried him past McAvoy in two steps, and as he raced for the back of the cabin, he smashed into Shorty Evans, grabbed him and wrestled him to the mud. "As far as you go, Doolin," he growled. He was about to smash his revolver across the man's head when Evans shouted at him.

"Damn, Shorty, I'm sorry. Never did see who you were until you said something." The two were getting up from a deep mud puddle when McAvoy showed up.

"Murphy's coming around the building from the other side. He thinks Doolin is inside already," Evans said. They ran around the building and met up with Murphy who was kneeling over Anderson's dead body.

"He's inside with Mrs. Anderson and Snider," Murphy said. "McAvoy, you stay with me, and Corcoran, you and Shorty get to the other side. Watch those window gun slits, and let's kill that bastard. We got to keep him from that woman." He looked around and asked, "Where's Jake Oxford?"

"He's okay," McAvoy said. "Tore his knee up bad falling down the steps in the barn. He'll be with us." Murphy nodded and motioned everyone off.

Shorty and Corcoran were able to duck under the window slit on the west side of the building and knock more of the fire down, but the wall was just about fully involved, and the flames were menacing the roof overhang. "That roof will burn hot and fast, Shorty. If we're gonna save Beverly and get her and Snider out of there, it's gonna have to be quick."

"One good kick at that door and it'll crumble into ash, Corcoran. Before we make any kind of move, we gotta know where the three of them are."

"Yeah. I'm thinkin' they're probably on the other side of the house. This fire's hot, and there's lots of smoke. I'm gonna see if I can see anything," and he ducked low to get up to the window slit. The shutter covering the window and the walls were made from heavy timbers, and Corcoran didn't think a bullet would go all the way through.

He eased himself up to see through the slit without showing much of his head. "All I can see is smoke," he said, ducking down from the window. "Ain't gonna be nobody in that part of the house."

Shorty Evans walked up to the burning door and gave it a solid kick sending flaming and smoking chunks of the door in several directions. Two shots rang out immediately, one hitting Shorty in his right arm, knocking him to the ground. "Damn," he shouted through the pain. Corcoran ran to grab him and pull him well off to the side of the house.

"Not my smartest move, Corcoran, but at least you will have a better look now." Evans tried to rip his shirt open, and Corcoran did it for him, wadded the shreds up and put it over the wound.

"Hold that in place until the bleeding stops. You might be right about being able to see in, but Doolin can see out just as well." Corcoran's usual good humor failed him. "Damn it, Shorty, you're out of the fight now unless you're as good with your left hand as you are with your right. That was a fool's move."

"I'm sorry don't make it, I know, but even though it hurts like hell, I think I can still use my right hand. I'll cover any move you make. Help me tie this off."

"Right now, I got no move to make," the big redhead growled. He ripped more of Shorty's shirt and tied the bloody pad in place. "Let me see you flex your fingers, Shorty." Shorty held his hand up, flexed his fingers with the slightest groan. "Good," Corcoran said. He got up and moved back toward the partially destroyed door.

. . .

Doolin was in an awkward spot now, and for a change, he knew it. The house was on fire, there were people outside looking to kill him, and he was alone with the woman he had plans for. She, however, had plans as well, and he found that out quickly. He had her by the arm just inside the back room of the cabin when the front door exploded in. He whirled, pulling his revolver, and fired two rounds as quick as he could, but he had to let go of her to do that. His bad arm just hung useless at his side.

Beverly jumped free and ran for the back door. Doolin screamed "No!" And jumped at her, knocking her to the floor again. He howled in pain when he fell on his wounded shoulder, couldn't grab her without letting go of the pistol, and slapped her across the side of her head with the gun. The pain seared, blood flowed from the now open wound, and Doolin felt almost helpless.

Beverly's head was bleeding hard, and she was almost unconscious. She felt herself being dragged across the rough floor, tried to fight but was too weak. She felt Doolin trying to rip more of her clothes off, squirmed, kicked, but to no good. He was too strong, and she was badly hurt from the whacks to her head.

"Bitch," he growled, getting up on his feet. He dragged her almost unconscious body over to the wall, ripped her skirt off and used it to tie her arms behind her back. "You're gonna like what comes next," he snickered. He dragged her to the bed, wasn't able to lift her, and spent a full minute cussing at the top of his lungs.

"You're mine, woman. If you want it on the floor, so be it," he screamed, kicked her hard in the ribs, and started trying to get out of his clothes.

. . .

"Hear that?" Murphy had McAvoy up against the door with him. "There's something going on in there." He slowly moved his fingers around the lever to open the door and found it locked in place. "Must have a bolt to hold that," he muttered. He rattled it hard to see if he could dislodge the bolt, but the lever held solidly in place. "Damn.

McAvoy worked his way down the wall to the gun slit and slowly brought his eye up to it. He almost jumped back by what he saw. "Sumbitch is gonna rape Beverly," he howled his anger. He pulled his pistol, aimed it through the slit and fired blindly into the room.

"Stop!" Murphy yelled out. "Snider's in there, too, McAvoy. Let's take a minute and work this out. This isn't the time to let your anger take over." They stepped back from the building, slightly to the side of the gun slot.

"Sorry, but that lady is like a daughter to me. I can't just stand by and let that killer have her. I ain't that good at thinkin', Sheriff, but I'm damn good at doin'."

"Let's make sure the doin' ain't killin' our own people. Now calm down and let's put together a plan to whup on that boy."

Doolin had his pants down around his boot tops when the gunshot rang out, and a bullet tore through the bed's mattress, just inches from his naked knee. Instinct took over, and he rolled out from the bed and across the floor, reaching back for his gun belt, on the floor next to the bed.

He jumped to his feet, working hard to get his pants

back up, and with just one hand working, couldn't fasten the buttons. He grabbed the pistol from its leather and stormed to the window slot. He couldn't see anyone but stuck the pistol through the slot and fired it.

Murphy saw the gun barrel come through the slot and quickly brought his rifle up and fired just as the pistol went off. The rifle shot hit the pistol at the cylinder, and the gun all but exploded in Doolin's hands, driving him back onto the cabin floor. His face was bleeding from scattered wounds and one eye missing. The hot metal was still burning flesh in some wounds, and Doolin was screaming, thrashing about, raking his face.

The force of the explosion ripped great chunks of meat from his hand, broke bones, adding to his other problems. He was whimpering when Beverly started to regain consciousness.

"My God, what's happened?" She looked about the room, heard, then saw, Doolin on the floor in a fetal position, whimpering like a baby. His pants were down around his knees, and there was blood everywhere. It was then she noticed the slightest movement from Aaron Snider.

"My God," she said again, rushing to his side. "You're alive." She saw that the wounds were to the side of his body, not the middle as she had thought.

"Let's get you up on that bed," she said. He motioned to the floor near her feet. She was busy trying to get him up, and he resisted again, trying to point at the floor. He was too heavy for her, and she finally looked at where he was pointing. "The gun," she whispered and reached down to grab it, but Doolin was faster, grabbing for the pistol but not being able to hold on to it. Broken bones and torn flesh weren't working.

He had no strength in one hand because of the severe

shoulder wound, and his other hand was useless from the exploding pistol. Beverly was able to wrench the gun from wounded fingers and jumped back away from the outlaw. She was trembling, more frightened than she had ever been, holding a gun aimed at the man who killed her husband.

Everything in her was screaming, "kill the bastard," but killing a man in cold blood wasn't in her. She held the gun in both hands, aimed at the middle of his head. She struggled to pull the hammer back, aimed again, had her finger on the trigger, but couldn't do it. Doolin saw that right away and started to get on his feet, get that gun back, kill these people and run.

He couldn't walk because his pants were hanging at his knees and instead lunged, and she couldn't pull the trigger. He plunged into her, knocking the gun away as the two fell to the floor. Doolin's hands and arms were useless, but he was big, and he rose and fell on the woman twice, knocking the air out of her, before starting to get to his feet. "Bitch," he snarled, holding the gun loosely by just one finger. "I'll kick your brains out, stomp on that pretty face, kill you," he screamed.

She was thrashing about on the floor, trying desperately to stay away from the insane man who was trying to kick her brains out. She could feel the heat from the burning kitchen, and was wild with fear, tried to get to her feet but was again thrown to the floor when the man fell on her. *The door,* she *thought, I've got to get to the door.* She was on her hands and knees, only in her bloomers, fighting to reach the door.

"There's all kinds of a ruckus going on in that other room,

Shorty," Corcoran said, standing to the side of the burning doorway. "I'm going in, cover me as best you can or follow." He was looking through a wall of fire as the entire kitchen seemed to be burning.

"I'm with you, Corcoran," Shorty Evans said.

Corcoran held his arm across his face and leaped through the flaming doorway into the large kitchen and raced for the door leading to the back room. Smoke was thick and putrid, and he was coughing hard when he burst into the other room. Pieces of the burning door flew out into the room. His eyes were watering, he could hardly see, and ducked down, jumping to the side, just in case he could be seen.

He wiped his eyes quickly and saw Snider on the bed, bleeding heavily, Beverly was on the floor looking up at Doolin who was holding a pistol with just one finger. He covered the distance between them in two steps, bashing the outlaw across the head with his heavy Colt, driving the man face first onto the floor.

Corcoran kicked Doolin hard in the ribs and helped Beverly to her feet and onto the bed. He walked to the back door and undid the bolt. "It's me, Corcoran, opening the door. Don't shoot the good guy," he yelled out and opened the door. "We need to get these people to the barn before the house burns down around us."

Beverly was still feeling the effects of being bashed on the head and kicked in the ribs more than once but got busy putting together the important things to be saved. "There's a strong box in the kitchen," she said. "Money, important papers. I've got to get that."

Corcoran took her hand and helped her back to the bed. "I'll get it," he said. The kitchen was fully involved, but Corcoran had been in more than one burning building in his long career, knew the only breathable air was down at floor level and got down on the floor. He had to crawl across the bare wood floor, now almost as hot as the walls, to the stove. "About twelve feet over there, I guess," he muttered, snaking across the floor. Flames were crackling all around him, burning chunks of wood were falling to the floor and onto his back as he moved as fast as he could.

He found the heavy iron box and was dragging it back when a large section of the roof collapsed, falling on top of him. He knew his clothing was on fire, he could smell burning flesh as well, felt pinned, squirmed free, and started rolling as hard as he could toward the open door. The pain was fierce, the smoke choking, and he was having trouble breathing and seeing. He had a death hold on the strong box.

Murphy raced into the inferno and grabbed Corcoran by his boots, pulling him into the back room. He got him far from the kitchen flames and slapped at the open flames burning Corcoran's clothes. "Easy, old man," Corcoran coughed out. "That's my face you're beating on."

"Been wanting to for a while now," Murphy chuckled. "You're a mess."

Beverly grabbed Corcoran and hugged him tight. "Let's get you cleaned up, Terrence." She was crying, getting him to his feet and onto the bed. She was wiping his face, tears running down hers.

"That can wait," he said, gently pushing her hands away. "We need to get everyone out to the barn before this house comes down on top of us." He had to laugh, looking around at the group, standing in the middle of a burning house.

"Just look at us. Bev, half dressed, Snider bleeding hard, me burnt up. Let's get moving before we die." McAvoy was next to Beverly in an instant, had her wrapped in a blanket, telling her she was safe now. "Where the hell are Shorty Evans and Jake Oxford?"

"We're here," Jake called from outside. "Shorty found me in the mud and helped me. Where'd Doolin?"

"He's not quite dead, yet," Corcoran said. Let's get moving."

The heat was intense, and flames had taken complete hold of the roof and walls as they grabbed what they could and moved toward the barn. Murphy had Doolin slung over his shoulder, and Shorty Evans and McAvoy had Beverly and Snider between them. Oxford was limping hard trying to help Corcoran get through the mud and out to the barn.

"I sure hope you brought that magic medicine of yours, Beverly. This bunch is a seriously messed up posse." Corcoran was coughing and laughing at the same time. He was helping Jake Oxford get into the barn more than the young deputy was helping him. "Murphy, you're gonna have your work cut out, getting this bunch back to civilization."

Everyone pitched in and did what they could to establish a camp of sorts at the barn. Clint McAvoy's existing camp was the starting point. "Snider and Doolin are hurt the most," Murphy said. "To hell with Doolin. If he dies, so be it, but let's tend to Snider right away."

Beverly Anderson went to work on the young deputy but could see that his wounds were of the worst kind. "Those bullets tore up his insides, Terrence," she said, tears running down her filthy face. "All we can do is try to make him comfortable. Let's get started on your burns. Turn around, big boy."

It was the first time he'd seen her smile, and he did

what he was told. He turned, and she used what was left of her dress, which she brought with her out of the cabin but never put back on, to clean the burned back. He couldn't help giving a solid grunt or two and then she spread the ointment over the burns. "That stuff's amazing," Corcoran said, slipping into a clean shirt. "Sucks the pain right out of you."

"I need to take care of Silas, Terrence," Beverly whispered.

He wrapped his arms around the lady and held her tight. She was gasping, crying, trying not to scream. "We will, Bev, I promise. He'll be taken care of properly. He kept his arms around her and let her sob into his shoulder. "He was a good man, Bev, and he died protecting you." He got up slowly and motioned for Jake Oxford to come over.

"She needs a friend right now, Jake. I've seen your work on Doolin and Snider, and you have a way about you. She's busted up physically and mentally. Take care of her."

Jake Oxford sat down in the straw and let Beverly stretch out some. "Your ribs need to be bound up, Beverly. I'll be as tender as I can, but it's gonna hurt. I'll need to clean up those gashes in your pretty head, too." He had her chuckling just a bit as he worked on her wounds. He talked to her the whole time he was mending the problems.

"Are you sure my Silas is dead? I know he was shot."

"I'm afraid so. We'll do the right thing when the sun comes up. Right now, we need to take care of you. Mr. McAvoy will have my head if I don't get you well taken care of." She couldn't hold the chuckles back, and squeezed his hand, trying to smile through the hurt.

"Clint has always been the one take care of me, Jake, but I like the way you do, too. What am I going to do?

The cattle and hogs need to be made ready for market, the house is gone," she started crying again, and Jake Oxford simply wrapped her in his arms and let her sob.

What is she going to do? A woman, alone in this huge valley? Just an old man working for her? My, God, what is she going to do? Jake Oxford's knee hurt more the longer he sat on the hard dirt floor, but with his arms wrapped around Beverly Anderson, he didn't really care.

CHAPTER EIGHTEEN

"It'll be light soon," Corcoran said, helping Murphy get Doolin tied tight. The outlaw was still alive but was unconscious. His shoulder was seriously infected, gangrene obvious to all who got near. "We're a hundred miles from the nearest doctor, Murph. Ain't no way he can stay alive until we get there."

"We caught him, Corcoran. That's the only thing that counts. I just hope we can keep Mr. Snider alive for that doc to see. Belly wounds are killers. He's a good man, a good deputy."

"We've got a long way to go to get all of us back to Eureka, and most of us wounded." Beverly had cleaned and dressed the burns on his back, and he felt as good as new. "Let's all sit by the fire for a few minutes and put our situation on the table. We're not in trouble, but we could be if we don't make the right moves these next few days."

"I know you won't pay any attention, but you need to calm down, Terrence," she said. "There are plenty of people here to see to it that things get done. Let your back heal; let your head heal."

He laughed a bit and took her hand and kissed it. "Might say the same to you, little darlin'. You are one beat-up woman, and you're gonna need all the rest and all the help you can get. Those ribs of yours are gonna hurt like all the demons are inside fightin', and your pretty little head needs some soft and tender strokin'."

"You just take your blarney down the road, Terrence Corcoran," she laughed. "But I wish part of that might come true."

"We've got two wagons, Corcoran." Clint McAvoy interrupted. He had been tending Beverly since they made their way to the barn and felt this was a good time to break up their little conversation. A good fire was lit, coffee was brewed, and they even took a little time to eat. "We need to take enough time to tend to everyone's wounds before wandering off across the valley."

"I don't give a damn whether Doolin lives or dies on the road back," Murphy said, "but as to the others, I agree. Let's make sure we are able to make the journey."

Snider was the most seriously wounded of the posse members, and Beverly was suffering from concussion and deep cuts to her head along with broken ribs. Corcoran's back was badly burned, and Jake Oxford was sure there was something broken in his knee. "We'll take the rest of today to tend to wounds, make sure the wagons are ready, put together food and supplies, and leave out of here at daybreak tomorrow," Corcoran said.

"It's at least sixty miles north to the wagon road that will take us into Eureka. We'll need food for at least five days. That would give us a little insurance in case we run into trouble along the way."

"We should stop to resupply at the Pine Ranch," McAvoy said. "They're good people."

"I know they'll welcome us. Mrs. Pine is good at doctoring, too," Beverly said. "Clint, show Sheriff Murphy where we keep our smoked and barreled meat. We'll need it for this long trip."

Beverly motioned Corcoran to walk with her. "I doubt that Mr. Snider will make that kind of journey, Terrence. The bullets went into his side but didn't come out. It tore through his insides something horrible. I've got the bleeding stopped, but I'm sure, with our summer heat, that gangrene will set in real soon."

"I'm feeling the same about Doolin. He's got so many serious wounds, already showing signs of infection that he'll be dead in a day. I'm worried about you, little darlin'. Your eyes aren't exactly working as a team," he chuckled. "You can't focus, can you?"

"Not really," she smiled, but her eyes said there was pain behind them. "I've got a raging headache." She put her arms around Corcoran, and he held her tight, letting her cry for as long as she wanted.

"Can we bury Silas?" She whimpered, her knuckles white and her fingers digging into Corcoran's back. "We had a day-to-day fight to keep this place going. He never complained, never gave a thought to giving up. He was the most wonderful man I ever met, Terrence." Her whimpering became full-blown blubbers, and Corcoran walked her out of the barn and over to a large cottonwood tree.

"Let's sit in the grass for a minute or two, Bev. You're suffering from concussion, and it's hard to think, I know, but you've got some mighty serious thinking coming your way. I'll take care of Silas right away, but what are you gonna do? You've got a section of land under homestead, it's yours now, and it's more than one person can take care of."

"I know, Terrence. I know," she cried. "I won't give it up. I won't. Clint has always been like a father to me, and I know if I ask he'll stay. I would need one more man, young and strong, like you, Terrence. Not to be a husband, I don't think I'll ever want another husband, but to work with Clint and me."

"You're a young and attractive woman, Beverly. You'll have young men strung out from here to Carson City, wanting an opportunity to work for you." Her eyes danced a little, and there was actually a chuckle along, too. "It wouldn't surprise me if Jake Oxford doesn't apply before our trip is over."

She tried to laugh and coughed instead. "He's mighty good looking but kind of young, I think." And she blushed and tried to turn from Corcoran who held her tight, laughing right out. "You know what I mean," she stammered, and he laughed even more.

"You're gonna be fine, little darlin'."

Yes, I am and so is my ranch. Poor Silas. I love you, Si, and it was your anger that done you in. Your anger and that damn calf, and we don't have no babies, and I haven't had a man in more years than I can count.

It was a solemn group that stood around Silas Anderson's grave later that day. Giles Murphy read from the singed pages of Anderson's bible that had survived the fire, and they even sang a hymn to send the man off. "This won't be the last, I'm afraid," Murphy said. "You worried about Aaron Snider, Corcoran?"

"Yup. Can smell the gangrene. His guts were opened up, Murph. He's a tough one, but not that tough. Makes me damn angry to know I can't do anything for him. Just sit and watch him suffer. I won't do it, but I'd like to shoot him and get his suffering over."

"It would be the kind thing to do, but we both know it can 't be done. We'll pull out in the morning. Jake can drive a wagon even if he can't walk," Murphy chuckled, "and Shorty can drive the other one. "We'll put Snider in one and Doolin in the other, and bury them on the trail in, I'm afraid."

The rest of the day was busy, getting what food they could find in the remains of the cabin and the smokehouse packed up. They loaded the wagons with everything except their own bedrolls and took care of the wounded. Corcoran found Beverly standing near the front of the burned-out cabin.

"I'll rebuild, Terrence. I will." She pointed out across the wide valley. The mountains to the west stood almost nine thousand feet high and were still topped by fields of snow despite the summer heat below. "Six hundred and forty of those acres are mine, now. I'm going to put in claims for more and grow that herd. I'm young and strong and I ain't gonna be beat by that miserable outlaw."

"I saw you going through the rubble. Were you able to save anything?"

"We didn't have much," she laughed. "It was just us. All my clothes burned, I'm afraid, and our furniture. Silas made a lot of that. God, I'll miss that man."

It was quiet around the campfire that night, and they slept with their own thoughts about this strange journey across the state, chasing a stupid outlaw and losing a good man.

Beverly wrapped herself in a blanket and got as close to the fire as she dared, looking out across the prairie. *Been here looking at those mountains for so many years and always able to feel the strong muscles of my man, holding me tight. I haven't slept alone for more than ten years, haven't had to make serious decisions about life for even longer. That young deputy has all the makings of a fine man, a good man, and I'm going to need one of those.* She was fast asleep in minutes, the blankets soaking up the heat of the fire along with some of her's.

"Looks like we have one nasty chore before we harness the teams, Murphy," Corcoran said, nudging the man awake. "Snider didn't make it. He took a bullet that shouldn't have even been fired. Beverly said he saved her life in the cabin, and we have to leave him here. There are times, Murphy, that I don't like my job."

"Make the coffee, Corcoran, and we'll bury one of my best deputies. He was a town boy, loved walking the streets, didn't much care for horses, couldn't rope a fence post, but would do anything I asked. I'm gonna miss him, Corcoran, for a long time."

Silas was buried on a slight rise several hundred feet back from the burned out cabin, near a copse of pine trees. Beverly asked that Aaron Snider be buried alongside her husband. "He was a good man, Terrence. I'm alive because of him." The group stood quiet, a few words were said, and the thoughts of getting on the road were in everyone's mind.

"Silas and I ran away to get married and start this ranch," Beverly said as they walked back to the barn from the graves. "Now, I have a ranch with two graves. I don't know if I'm strong enough for this, Terrence."

"I'd bet a month's wages on it," Corcoran said. "You, little darlin' are one tough lady."

"That's it, Corcoran," McAvoy said. "This is now the One Tough Lady ranch. And, by damn, I'm the foreman."

Tensions were eased by that comment, but they weren't able to get on the road for another hour or so. It was a quiet line of riders and wagons that finally moved off the One Tough Lady ranch. "We'll fight thunderstorms every afternoon, Murph. It's the way of the high mountain desert in the middle of summer."

"Yeah, and we'll bury another before we reach that wagon road, too, I fear."

Murphy was wrong. Doolin not only wouldn't die but Beverly was able to keep most of his wounds under control. Infections cleared up, scabs weren't torn loose, and the man was miserable company at all times. He complained every hour he was alive, to the point they put him in the trail wagon and only Shorty Evans could stay with him, put up with him. "I'll not shoot the sumbitch, but I can be just as nasty as he."

Doolin demanded water and Shorty told him to go to hell. He demanded the wagon not go so fast over the bumpy trail and Shorty put the ponies in a trot. He seemed to try to work his way out of his bonds every hour he was awake.

"He may not be in quite as much pain as he's making us believe," Shorty Evans told Murphy the third day out. Murphy growled to just tie him tighter. The miles stretched out in an endless ribbon to follow.

Beverly also tended Corcoran's burns and had them healed enough that he felt comfortable in just a day or two. "You've got more scars than I've ever seen on one person, Terrence. You need to take better care of yourself. You need a woman, Terrence."

"I came close, once," Corcoran said, the thoughts of

Betsy fighting through the haze of memory. "I'm a wanderer, Beverly, always will be. I call Eureka my home, but Ed Connors will tell you I will use any excuse to take off, just like this. I'm chief deputy. I could have had one of the other men join this posse, but, oh no, it was gonna be me," he chuckled.

"How are you and Jake getting along? His knee gonna heal up?"

She ducked her head and blushed some before answering. "He's a fine man, Terrence. I've asked him to consider going to work at the ranch."

"You need a man like Jake. It might take a little time, but I'm sure you two will find love and that ranch will continue. I'm getting mighty personal, Beverly, but why didn't you and Anderson have any children?

"He couldn't father a child." She had her eyes cast down so he couldn't see the tears that were forming. "He was gored badly not long after we were married and..." she sobbed, and Corcoran took her in his arms.

"I'm sorry. It's none of my business." He rubbed her back, let her cry. "Maybe Jake Oxford is exactly what you need." He smiled feeling her fingers dig deep into his shoulders.

"It's been so long, Terrence, but I don't want to think about that now. Me and Silas had such plans, such dreams, ruined by this man we're fighting so hard to keep alive. Our ranch is at stake now. All our work burned to the ground; cattle strung out for miles.

"I'm a wreck, Terrence. What am I going to do?"

"I think I'd send Clint McAvoy back to the ranch to start rebuilding. You're on your way to Eureka to settle all the legal stuff. I'd grab hold of Jake Oxford and hang on tight. I know everything is happening so fast, but your life is at stake here. You can't ever bring Silas back, all you can do is keep his memory alive.

"But you have to live, Beverly and that big strong young man is the answer for you right now."

"You've always been my friend, Terrence. I'll have a talk with Jake. He is one of the nicest men I've ever met, but... well, I'll have a talk with him," she said. She was chuckling as she turned her face away from Corcoran.

She'll do fine. Jake Oxford is a good lawman, but he'll be a much finer rancher having a lovely lady like that at his side.

From the Anderson's to the Pine's was forty miles but they were lucky to make eight miles in a day, and the trail was taking its toll on everyone. Beverly called Clint McAvoy to her side that night for a long chat.

"We should be at Gene Pine's place tomorrow, Clint, and I need to know that you're still my number one man on the ranch. I can't imagine trying to run that place without you."

"I'm afraid you'd have to shoot me to get me off the place, little lady. I'd feel mighty good if you'd tell me to turn around and go back right now."

She could feel the weight lift from her shoulders, smiled, and settled a little closer to the fire. "No, not tonight, but after we get to the Pine's, I think, would be a good time to head back."

Clint McAvoy had a quick mind, didn't know too much about the ins and outs of men and women and love and all that but did know what he had been seeing the last couple of days. "You talked to that young boy?"

"I don't know what you mean," she said, a bit too quickly.

"I ain't gonna try to spell it out, Beverly, cuz I wouldn't know what to say. You got eyes for him, and he's got eyes for you. You need him at the ranch, and he wants to be there."

"I've asked Jake to work for me, Clint. What else happens... well, we'll just have to wait and see."

She smiled into the fire and McAvoy had a smile as he walked to the back wagon to grab his bedroll.

CHAPTER NINETEEN

Gene Pine rode up to the group as they moved off the trail and onto the pathway leading to his generous ranch house. The Pine ranch was a full three sections in the valley and Pine, along with his wife, Barbara, ran many hundreds of head of cattle, sheep, and hogs. He drove his animals northwest to Eureka where they were slaughtered or shipped to the more populated areas of the west.

Pine spotted Beverly riding off to Corcoran's side. "What have we here?" He said in greeting.

"Evening, Mr. Pine," Corcoran said. "Some bad doin's I'm afraid." He told the story as they rode up to the ranch house. Gene's wife, Barbara met them at the kitchen door, and the story was told again as the walking wounded were moved off the wagons or down from saddles.

Barbara Pine was a southern woman who came west as a youngster when her family felt the need to leave Georgia as the war between the states seemed imminent. Gene Pine was moving cattle in New Mexico Territory when her family was traveling to California. He was a strapping twenty-year-old, and she was a fifteen-year-old, slightly plump girl who loved horses and cattle.

They were among the first to homestead this long, generously watered valley in the wilds of Nevada Territory. She has worked right alongside her husband for all the years, raised one boy who left home at fifteen, telling them he hoped he never saw another cow. There two hired hands have been with them for years.

"Oh, my, that's just terrible," Barbara Pine exclaimed after hearing about Doolin, the fire, and the killing of Silas Anderson. She knew there were outlaws but had never seen one or been as close to one as she was at this moment. "Oh, Beverly, I'm so sorry." She hustled around the kitchen for a minute, gathering a few items. "Come, dear, let's get you cleaned up. You men do what's necessary for that outlaw, just don't bring him in my home. Of all the horrible things you've just told me, I won't have that man dirtying my home."

"He needs help, Barbara," Gene Pine said. Pine had never had an enemy in the world, was a friend to anyone needing help, and Barbara often said he would give his shirt away in the middle of a blizzard if someone else needed it.

"Then help him into the hog wallow, not my home." Gene had to chuckle at the comment, saw the fear in her eyes, and knew better than to argue the point. She took Beverly by the arm and led her upstairs and into one of the bedrooms. "Of all the things," she said several times. "What are you going to do, Beverly? You can't run that ranch by yourself."

Beverly straightened her shoulders some and looked long and hard at this strong ranch wife telling her she couldn't do something she's been doing right along. "I most certainly can run that ranch. I have been working right alongside Silas from our first day on that land. My goodness, Barbara, after all, I have Clint McAvoy and will hire another one or two men. No, Barbara, I'm not giving up what I've worked so hard to have."

She paced around the room for a moment, wondering where that comment came from. "After all, Barbara, you work right next to Gene. I'm staying," she said. *Would she give up the Pine ranch if something happened to Gene? I'm sure she works at least as hard as I do on this ranch, loves it as much as I do mine. Stupid question.*

Barbara ignored the strong response and called for the woman who cooks and cleans for the ranch. "Angie. Get the tub filled with hot water. This dear child needs a scrubbing from top to bottom." The lady, married to one of the buckaroos and almost part of the family, scurried downstairs. "I can't seem to get it all in my head. Silas, dead. Your beautiful little cabin burned to the ground." She stopped suddenly and just stared at Bev. "Oh, my goodness. Of course you're staying. What a stupid thing for me to say." She was wringing her hands, pacing about.

"You're a strong woman, Beverly. I hope you know that Gene and I will always be here for you. Now, without meaning anything nasty, little lady, you're a mess, filthy, and you must be terribly tired. Let's get you in a hot bath, some clean bedclothes, and Into bed for a long sleep."

"I haven't slept much since that night, Barbara. Thank you."

She melted in a large tub filled with steaming water and cried great sobs wondering how much worse life could get. She could feel Silas next to her when she climbed into a large bed and hoped that feeling would never go away. *Terrence Corcoran is trying to mate me up with that young deputy and Barbara is trying to tell me I can't run that ranch. They're both wrong. Jake Oxford will be a good hand, and he's probably going to end up being my husband, but not yet. The One Tough Lady Ranch will earn its name.* The smile remained on her face for the entire nap.

"Where we gonna put this outlaw? Can't just throw him to the hogs, even if Mrs. Pine might want us to?" Gene Pine was chuckling, watching Sheriff Murphy and Shorty Evans haul Brad Doolin out of the wagon. "All I see is blood. Is he alive?"

"He's breathing," Murphy said. "Got room in the barn?" He and Evans laid Doolin out on the ground while they talked the matter over. "Hog pen might not be a bad idea, though. Don't know if the hogs would want something this ugly." The chuckles went around among the men.

"Barn'll be fine," Pine said. "I got an empty stall with straw down. He looks like he's been shot just about everywhere."

"I think so," Corcoran said. "Man's too dumb to know it's time to die. He wasn't worth a tobacco plug before, and if he lives, he'll be worth even less. There are times I don't much care for being a responsible person. It'd be so easy to just let him be, so he can die."

"Corcoran, what I've heard, you've always done the right thing," Pine said. There was uproarious laughter at that point, and Terrence feigned throwing a couple of fists at the men. "Okay," Pine continued, "let's drag him to the barn. It'll be you boys taking care of him. I know Barbara won't help." He looked up at the house and back down at Doolin, and just shook his head.

"Make yourselves comfortable, Corcoran. We usually have supper around sunset."

"Let's get him in the barn, Shorty," Murphy said.

Corcoran watched Shorty and Murphy man-handle Doolin into the barn. *Don't make much sense sometimes. Got us a killer, a man who has murdered lawmen, women, wounded a child, and we catch him. He should hang, right now. And we have to molly-coddle the bastard. Should simply kill the man but can't because he should get a trial. It's the law, and I respect the law.*

Well, I guess they're right, and it is the law. Our country is built on the rule of law, and if it's good for one, it must be good for all. He kicked some dust walking across the large barnyard, back toward the big house Pine had built. *Right here on this place, there is the scum of society bleeding in the barn, and there's a man who settled this valley and made a good life for his family. Opposite ends of the social spectrum. I could sure use a cold beer right about now.*

Corcoran motioned for Clint McAvoy to walk with him. "We got to think about Beverly now, Clint. There's no reason for you to ride on into Eureka with us. I'll take good care of the little lady. You need to be back at that ranch."

"Thank you, Corcoran. We talked about that, and I'll head back at first light," he chuckled. "I love that pretty girl, and I know the ranch is where I belong right now. She's gonna need more help, though. Silas did one heap of work around that place."

"I'm not sure, but I think she's already talked with Jake Oxford about just that," Corcoran said. McAvoy got a quick smile and nodded. "Murphy and Evans have Doolin laid out on a bed of straw in a stall, and Jake's been doing a good job doctoring this fool." Corcoran got a snarl in his voice, and McAvoy saw his jaw tighten.

"They ain't a judge in the country that wouldn't hang the bastard, and here we are doing everything possible to keep him alive."

"Whenever you get life all figured out, Corcoran, you let me know, eh?" McAvoy whopped the big deputy across the shoulders. "Men and women, cattlemen and sheepmen, lawmen and outlaws. Hell, Corcoran, you'll get it figured out." The two were laughing when Oxford walked up on them.

"Miss something?" He looked around with a smile. "Looks like every wound on that dumb outlaw is bleeding again."

"Old man Corcoran here was doing a bit philosophyin', Jake. He's lookin' to get a handle on life."

"I got a handle on my life," Jake said. A smile crept across his young face followed immediately by shades of red. He stammered around several words and finally just stood in front of the two older men with a big dumb look on his face.

"I gather you had a talk with Beverly," Terrence said.

"I did. My goodness she's pretty," he said, and the blush returned. "I'm going to help her with all the legal stuff when we get to Eureka and then come back to work on the ranch. I'll be working with you, Clint, if that's all right with you."

"I'll put money on this, young Mr. Oxford. Within the year I'll be working for you," McAvoy chuckled. The blush could have been seen at the big house. Conversation came to an end with the clanging of the big dinner bell and the three men headed to the ranch house.

I sure hope he's right. She's so kind, so sweet, and the most lovely girl I've ever met. I've always known that someday I would find my woman, but not like this. Seeing her dead husband, actually helping to bury the good man and now... am I lusting after that man's wife? No, it isn't lust, but it will be wonderful if what Clint said comes true.

"Just leave him where he lays," Corcoran said, nodding his head back at Doolin. "We'll bring him scraps when we're through." Doolin was responsible for the deaths of three lawmen, and the last thing on earth that Corcoran would do would be to offer any kindness to the man. "The courts will have some fun with this one.

"He's murdered people in Humboldt, Lander, and Eureka Counties, along with a few lesser charges in each. Which jurisdiction gets to hang him first?" There was general laughter as they walked into the warm kitchen.

"My goodness," Giles Murphy said when Beverly walked in. "Looks like you're headed for the annual pie and ice cream ball." Barbara walked with her, both dressed in fine silks and satins, hair cleaned and shining, and faces filled with life.

"All I've had on for five days is a pair of Clint's old pants and a shirt that poor Mr. Snider had. Everything I owned, burned to ashes. That's something I have to do when we get to Eureka is buy new clothes, boots, kitchen stuff, bedding. Everything," she whimpered.

Barbara beat Jake Oxford to her side. "Now, now, Beverly. We'll have none of that. Tonight, we only think of the future. There'll be plenty of time to remember." She led Beverly to the table, and everyone got seated. "Angie tells me we got enough food for the entire army, so let's get settled."

CHAPTER TWENTY

Supper was eaten fast that night. Everyone was exhausted, and there was also some let-down, knowing the killer was caught, would never kill again. "I'm not sure that he's as immobile as he wants us to believe," Jake Oxford said as the men made their way toward the barn. "I think he can move a bit more than he's making us think."

"I don't know how he could, but you would know better," Murphy said. "Think we should tie him up?"

"Yes, I do," Beverly Anderson said. "From the neck. Barbara Pine is terrified the man is going to attack her, kill her husband, and burn the ranch. She's heard every story about that creature and is terrified."

"I'll have a talk with Gene," Corcoran said. "We'll be leaving tomorrow morning, and he can use this time to calm her down. Maybe we should think about tying him off, though."

"No," Jake Oxford said. "He'll be fine tonight, and we're leaving out in the morning, so we'll just keep a close eye on him."

"What did you see, Jake?" Corcoran had seen more

than one outlaw play opossum with him. "If he's mobile, even a little bit, he's damn dangerous."

"Both of his hands are ruined, but I've seen him flexing them. He has also been working his shot-up shoulder some and trying to move about."

"His feet are chained to the stall posts, so he won't be hightailin' it anywhere," Corcoran said. "Don't let him fool you, though. You get mighty close to him when you're tending those wounds of his."

Corcoran left to have his talk with Gene Pine and the men spread their bedrolls in fresh straw in the barn. They were fast asleep within minutes. They went to sleep with Corcoran's words. "Let's remember what Jake said. Don't walk up on that man without being prepared for anything. He's on his way to the gallows, so he doesn't have any fear of anything right now."

Oxford was first up in the morning and took a quick look at the prisoner before waking the crew. "Well, Mr. Doolin, how we doing this fine morning? You can't have a whole bunch more blood to give."

Doolin didn't move, and Oxford found this unusual. He was usually already awake and angry when he came to check. Corcoran's words flashed through his mind, and he stood back half a step and used his foot to nudge the man. Doolin was in a fetal position with his back to Jake and Jake gave him a little harder jab with the toe of his boot, and once again, Doolin didn't move.

"Come on, Doolin, wake up," he said. "We're moving out this morning. Gotta change those bandages. Wake up," he almost shouted.

Jake Oxford knelt down to see if the man was even breathing and Doolin whirled around and took a mighty swipe with a hay hook. Jake jumped back just in time to keep from having that hook slash his throat open. The hook skinned his cheek, though, opening a gash about three inches long. He rolled across the straw covered floor, pulled his pistol and shot Doolin through the middle of his forehead.

"Bastard!" He was shaking, couldn't get his weapon back in the holster, and just lay there in the straw. He was breathing hard, glared at the dead outlaw, and slowly untied his neckerchief. He slowly wadded it up and tried to stop the heavy bleeding as Corcoran and Murphy came racing into the stall. "Oh, oh, oh," Corcoran said, grabbing the rag and forcing it into the wound. "What happened here?"

"He feigned sleep, and when I bent down to see if he was even alive, he ripped me open with a hay hook. It was just reaction, but I shot him dead." He was still sitting in the straw and tried to get up, couldn't, and just slumped back down. "I'm sorry. It was just a reaction. Sorry," he mumbled.

"You did the right thing, Jake. In more ways than one, I think." Corcoran kneeled down to make sure the outlaw was dead.

Murphy stood up holding the bloody hay hook out for everyone to see. "Could have ripped right through your throat with this thing, boy. You got yourself some good reflexes. Well, one of our biggest questions is now answered. Let's have some good ranch food and set for a bit of pow-wow, shall we?"

Pine and Beverly came racing in from the kitchen when they heard the gunshot. Beverly saw Jake holding the bloody rag to his cheek and rushed to his side. "Jake, Jake," she cried out. "My God, what happened?" She threw her arms around the young deputy, almost crying out the words.

"It's just a scratch, Beverly, uh, Mrs. Pine. I'm fine." She took the rag from his hand and started cleaning the wound. Tears were running down her cheeks, her fingers were strong, but she felt as weak as a newborn.

"Come to the house. I have my ointment. Oh, Jake, don't get hurt." *My God, I've just lost my husband and found the man who will run my ranch, probably be my husband, and now, I've almost lost him. Please, Jake, don't get hurt. I need you so much.*

Corcoran could see the fear written deep in the lady's eyes, the sound of her voice, her actions with Oxford. He wondered if they hadn't already made plans far ahead of what he had been thinking.

It was a full breakfast that Barbara set out for the mob and they attacked it with enthusiasm. She was thrilled when Gene Pine told her that the outlaw was dead, would never be able to hurt her or the ranch. "Thank God," she moaned. "Gene, I've never been so frightened of anyone in my life."

"You know I'd never let anyone bring you harm," he said, wrapping his arms around her.

"Well," she said, "I'd best get the biggest and best breakfast on the table now." And it was. Apple smoked bacon, mounds of potatoes, platters of biscuits, more eggs than one could count, and coffee by the gallon.

"Barbara, that was wonderful," Murphy said. "You're lucky that I'm the Lander County Sheriff, cuz, Ma'am, if I was Eureka County Sheriff, I'd be investigating crime at your back porch mighty regular."

"Murph," Corcoran roared in laughter. "You're sounding like Jake." He sat back in his chair and rubbed his belly, smiling at Barbara. "But you might see me a little more often."

"Enough of that, now," Murphy said. His brows were knit, and everyone knew it was time to think about getting on with their trip. "We've had good sleep, good food, no longer have a prisoner, and we all need to be somewhere. Gene, you and Barbara have taken mighty good care of us. If there are any charges from our visit, please forward them to Lander County. No, wait. This started because Doolin was a Humboldt County fugitive. Send the bill to Frank Acord," he laughed.

"There won't be any charges, Murphy. It was our plea-sure, taking care of you all. Beverly has been our neighbor and friend for many years, and she will always be welcome here. Murphy nodded.

"We will bury Mr. Doolin wherever you want us to, Gene, then pack it up and be on our way."

"I'll take the extra wagon and leave out right away for the ranch, Beverly," Clint McAvoy said. "You'll have a new cabin to come home to, and all the animals will be fine, too. Take proper care of your business and come home."

"We will," she said, stopped quick, blushed slightly, and looked down at the napkin in her lap. It was a very quiet kitchen as the group slowly filed from. Jake's hand brushed hers, and she grabbed it, holding it as tight as possible. With heads slightly bowed, the two smiled at each other.

Jake's knee was still tender, so he drove the wagon filled with bedrolls, food, and other personal equipment, and the rest rode horses. It was much faster, and they hit the major east-west highway the second day out.

"Murphy, let's you and me ride on ahead and let Shorty

Evans and Jake Oxford bring Beverly and the wagon in. I've got a million reports to write, and you have that many wires to send out."

"Every northern county will be glad to hear from me," Murphy joked. They tied bedrolls on, filled their saddle bags with food and bid the others goodbye. "We'll be making good time, Shorty. You and Jake keep Beverly safe."

On the second day, Corcoran led Murphy down the main street of Eureka and pulled up in front of the sheriff's office. Sheriff Ed Connors walked out to greet them. "Get your man, Corcoran?"

"We did, Ed, we got him, but we don't have him. Buried him at the Pine ranch. Worst man I've run into in a long time, Ed."

They walked into the office and found both coffee and a filled flask of Kentucky's finest, chairs, and quiet. Murphy swilled his fast and headed for the telegraph office. "Sheriff Acord ain't gonna like my wire on the one hand, but he can tell that banker we do have at least some of his money."

"You just gonna lay it out that Jake Oxford ain't coming home?" Corcoran half-way had to chuckle thinking about it. Murphy just laughed and walked out the door.

Corcoran spent the next hour telling Connors the story of the chase and Doolin's death. "He was a bastard to the last second of his life, Ed. Chained up, shot to hell, and he still tried to kill Jake Oxford. Sure glad this is over."

"Well, that end of it's over. I'd like to meet this Oxford fella when he comes in. Might try to talk him into staying here."

"You won't pry him from Beverly Anderson, Ed. That man's in love."

"Glad you sent that Evans deputy in. I followed up and arrested Butch Clemons and that fast-talking cattle buyer. Some of the boys up the valley were able to read through the rebranding and reclaim their cattle. The rest were put on the auction block, and the money went to the school district."

"Good show, Sheriff. Beverly Anderson, Jake, and Shorty should be here in a few days. I'm gonna go find a cold beer and a hot bath, and in that order."

"Yeah, you need to," Ed Connors joked, holding his nose. "Cindy Payton's been asking about you. Wondering when you'd be back and all."

"She's about to find out."

It was Beverly Anderson who led the remains of the posse into Eureka three days later. Jake Oxford was driving the wagon and trailing Shorty Evans horse. Corcoran ran off the porch to welcome them. "Where's Shorty?"

"In the back of the wagon," Jake said. "Damn fool walked right up on a rattlesnake. Got him twice, once in each leg. He's hurtin' bad, Corcoran. Where's the doc's and I'll take him there."

"Doctor White's right next door here. Climb down, and we'll get him in there. Bev, see the green door, that's doc's. Let him know we're coming in. Oh, and welcome to Eureka."

She laughed, jumping from her horse and hurrying to Doctor White's. Corcoran helped Jake down from the wagon. "Knee still sore?"

"Fightin' off a mean damn snake and then fightin'

Shorty to get him helped some, and my knee is killin' me, Corcoran." They helped Shorty Evans out of the back of the wagon and had to carry him into the doctor's office. Both his legs were swollen, horribly colored, and Evans was incoherent. "He can be downright stupid when he wants to," Oxford said.

Ed Connors tried to help, and Murphy showed up about that time, too. "I'm losing deputies faster than old Acord," he tried to quip. "He gonna live, Doc?"

"Maybe," White said. "You folks can clear out and go about your business now, and I'll do what I can to keep him alive." Shorty's pants were already ripped wide open, and the doc could see the strike marks plainly. "How'd he get that second bite?"

"Instead of backing off and shooting the snake he tried to stomp on it," Jake Oxford said. "I had a hell of a time gettin' them separated so I could shoot the thing. We came as fast as we could but tendin' him and driving the wagon, well, it just took some time to get here."

"Beverly, why don't you take Jake over to the Bonanza and get him a cold beer and a room. That boy's about wore out, I think." She smiled and got him up from a chair and out the door.

Corcoran watched Beverly help Jake down from the porch, and they walked across the street to the cafe, holding hands. His knee was still about twice the size it should be. "It was a fine chase, Ed," Corcoran laughed, slapping the sheriff across the shoulders. "A fine chase indeed. It's my turn for a cold beer and hot bath, and maybe several minutes or days with the lovely Cindy Payton."

"I'm gonna head back to Austin," Murphy said. "When that fool gets well, send him home, will you, Ed? I've got more wires and messages to send out." Giles Murphy joined Connor and Corcoran in the Bonanza for a cold beer first.

"Looks like you and Corcoran removed a big danger from the lives of our people here in central Nevada. Good job." Ed Connors slapped a gold eagle on the bar. "When that one's gone I'll find another. You boys got it comin'."

"He killed a good man in Silas Anderson, Connors. Killed a couple of fine lawmen, destroyed a family in Austin, and died trying to kill another fine lawman." Corcoran snarled, sipping his beer. "Old Frank Acord lost another fine deputy as well, I think. Jake Oxford ain't never goin back to a tin badge, not with Beverly hanging onto his arm."

"That pretty much sums up our chase," Corcoran said. "It was a good chase."

A LOOK: DEATH STALKS THE DIAMOND VALLEY: A TERRENCE CORCORAN WESTERN

By Johnny Gunn

The rich ranches of the Diamond Valley north of Eureka, Nevada, are plagued by rustlers, the Bank of Eureka is being threatened by a gang of bank robbers, the Eureka County Sheriff is wounded chasing rustlers, and Terrence Corcoran is named acting Sheriff. What could possibly go wrong?

Winters in the high mountains of central Nevada can be fierce, with ridges above eight thousand feet, heavy snow snaps trees, hurricane winds blow trees down, and man and beast are not safe. A botched train robbery sends Corcoran and his posse chasing the killers, deep into the Cortez Range as the first major blizzard of the winter arrives.

Is Corcoran looking at two gangs, rustlers and bank robbers, or are they somehow connected? It is the connection that is confusing. The rustlers try to kill Corcoran and his posse. The bank robbers try to kill Corcoran and his posse, but it is the connection that allows Corcoran to win.

There's humor, danger, and just a touch of buckaroo romance in the sixth Terrence Corcoran Western.

AVAILABLE SEPTEMBER 2019

ABOUT THE AUTHOR

Reno, Nevada novelist, Johnny Gunn, is retired from a long career in journalism. He has worked in print, broadcast, and Internet, including a stint as publisher and editor of the Virginia City Legend. These days, Gunn spends most of his time writing novel length fiction, concentrating on the western genre. Or, you can find him down by the Truckee River with a fly rod in hand.

"it's been a wonderful life. I was born in Santa Cruz, California, on the north shore of fabled Monterey Bay. When I was fourteen, that would have been 1953, we moved to Guam and I went through my high school years living in a tropical paradise. I learned to scuba dive from a WWII Navy Frogman, learned to fly from a WWII combat pilot (by dad), but I knew how to fish long before I moved to Guam.

"I spent time on the Island of Truk, which during WWII was a huge Japanese naval base, and dived in the lagoon. Massive U.S. air strikes sunk thousands of tons of Japanese naval craft, and it was more than exciting to dive on those wrecks. In the Palau Islands, near Koror, I also dived on Japanese aircraft that had been shot down into the lagoons.